To:

From:

Date:

God loves me!

Every Day a Blessing

Published in Nashville, Tennessee, by Tommy Nelson. Tommy Nelson is a registered trademark of Thomas Nelson.

Written by Jean Fischer

Illustrated by Carolina Farías

Tommy Nelson titles may be purchased in bulk for educational, business, fund-raising, or sales promotional use. For information, please e-mail SpecialMarkets@ThomasNelson.com.

Library of Congress Cataloging-in-Publication Data

Nelson, Tommy.
 Every day a blessing : a year of God's love / Tommy Nelson.
     pages cm
  Summary: "Spend an entire year of discovering God's blessings and develop a lifetime of gratitude. God loves everyone, and one way He shows His love is through showering us with blessings! Whether it's with parents who love us, warm sunshine, or the ultimate blessing of His Son Jesus, God's love is everywhere. When kids see that God is the source of all blessings, it reminds them that all gifts truly do come from God. Children will learn to not only see God's blessings in happy days, but to see His loving hand in hard days as well. Developing a habit of giving thanks in all circumstances will lead children to a lifelong spirit of gratitude. Each devotion features a Scripture and a bite-sized message that will keep the attention of young minds. Devotions also have a takeaway to help children engage with the message and apply its meaning to their lives. Sweet, beautiful art featuring both modern and biblical figures is by Carolina Far, illustrator of the Jesus Calling
  ISBN 978-1-4003-2185-8 (hardback)
  1. Children—Prayers and devotions. I. Title.
  BV4870.N45 2014
  242'.62—dc23   2013024264

Printed in China

14 15 16 17 18 LEO 6 5 4 3 2 1

Every Day a Blessing

A Year of God's Love

DEVOTIONAL

A Division of Thomas Nelson Publishers

NASHVILLE   DALLAS   MEXICO CITY   RIO DE JANEIRO

O LORD, our Lord, your
majestic name fills the
earth! Your glory is higher
than the heavens. You have
taught children and infants
to tell of your strength.

PSALM 8:1-2

A Note to Parents

Children are a gift from the LORD.
PSALM 127:3

DEAR PARENTS,

God's blessings are everywhere. One of His greatest blessings is the children He has placed in your care! And few things are more enjoyable than sitting down with your little ones to learn about God's great love for us. In *Every Day a Blessing*, you will enjoy reading together about God's blessings that are showered upon us each and every day—even when life is difficult and things don't go our way.

Through adorable illustrations, Scripture, engaging text, and helpful takeaway thoughts and prompts, your children will learn that they always have so many things to be grateful for, that they have a reason to say, "Thank You, God, for blessing me!" every day of the year.

As God's love and blessings in your children's lives are highlighted on each page, you will discover *together* how God grows grateful hearts and how by recognizing our blessings, we can bless others as well.

Blessings, Blessings Everywhere

Every perfect gift is from God.
JAMES 1:17

DID YOU KNOW THAT GOD LOVES YOU? He shows you His love with blessings. Blessings are all the things God gives you to show that He is with you always and that He cares for you. God cares so much for you that He went before you and placed blessings all through your life. The person reading this to you is a blessing—a gift to you from God. You can see God's blessings in the sunshine, in the sky, in the green grass on the ground, and everywhere in between. God's blessings are all around you. They are in your house, at school, at the playground, and wherever you go. Finding a blessing is like discovering a treasure. It is God saying, "I love you!"

When you discover a blessing, what should you say?
"Thank You, God, for blessing me!"

Shine Your Light

Each of you has received a gift to use to serve others.
Be good servants of God's various gifts of grace.

1 PETER 4:10 NCV

JESUS TOLD A STORY ABOUT LIGHT. He asked, "What good is a light if you hide it under a bowl?" He said that every person is like a light. When we share our blessings with others, it is like shining our light on the world. But not sharing our blessings is like hiding our light under a bowl.

God gave you special skills because He loves you. He wants you to share your skills to help others. Are you good at making things? You could make cards or door decorations for people in nursing homes. Are you good at growing things? You could grow some vegetables to give away.

Whatever your skills, don't keep them hidden. Share them with others, and let your light shine.

Use one of your skills to bless someone's day.

Thank You, God, for Your many blessings!

God Is Everywhere

"I am with you, and I will protect you everywhere you go."
GENESIS 28:15

GOD ISN'T ONLY IN HEAVEN. He is everywhere! God has the amazing power to be everywhere all the time. Whether you are at home, at a friend's house, on the playground, or on a vacation far away, God is always with you. He promises to watch over you wherever you go.

God blesses you every day by being there. He is interested in everything you do. When you wake up in the morning, God is there. All day long, He goes with you everywhere. And when you go to sleep at night, God stays and watches over you.

Say, "Hello, God." He hears you. He is with you right now.

Play hide-and-seek with a friend. You can never hide so well that God can't find you!

I am grateful God is with me.

God, the Maker of Everything

In the beginning God created the sky and the earth.
GENESIS 1:1

DO YOU ENJOY MAKING THINGS? God does. In the very beginning, God made the daytime and nighttime. Water was all over the place back then, spilling and swishing around, so God separated it from the sky. He gathered the water into oceans. He made land pop up everywhere—mountains, valleys, hills, and fields. He made pretty flowers, green grass, and tall trees. God hung the moon and the sun in the sky, and He filled the sky with stars. He made birds to fly and fish and other sea creatures to live in the water. And then God made animals—tiny mice that squeaked; big, burly lions that roared; every kind of animal! And when God finished filling the earth with these treasures, He said, "This is good."

What is your favorite thing God created? Why?

5

God Made You!

*All the days planned for me were written in
your book before I was one day old.*

PSALM 139:16

GOD MADE THE VERY FIRST MAN AND WOMAN. Their names were Adam and Eve. Then God made more people. He kept making them, and He still adds new people to the world every day.

One day, God made you. Before He made you, He knew exactly who you would be. He knew the color of your eyes, hair, and skin. He knew if your hair would be curly or straight, if you would have freckles on your nose, and even if you could rub your tummy and pat your head at the same time! God knew who your parents would be and what you will be when you grow up. God loves you so much that He knows everything about you.

⭐ *Isn't it a blessing that God made you? Draw a picture of yourself. Give yourself a happy smile.*

God Can Do Anything

God's wisdom is deep, and his power is great.

JOB 9:4

ADDIE AND HER MOMMY WENT TO THE MOVIES. They saw a cartoon that had talking animals. The animals rode bicycles and went to school.

Afterward, Addie's mother wondered, "Could real animals do that?"

"Of course not," said Addie. "It's only pretend."

There are some things that animals and people cannot do no matter how hard they try. The only One who can do everything is God.

With God, anything is possible. He made the world and all of its people. He is everywhere all at the same time. He fills up the earth with many wonderful blessings for you to discover. Do you know anyone else who can do that?

⭐ *Name three things your parents can do that you can't. Now try to name three things that only God can do.*

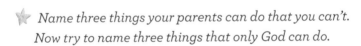

I'm so thankful God made me. He can do anything!

Jesus Loves Me

Jesus said, "Let the little children
come to me. Don't stop them."
MATTHEW 19:14

SOPHIA AND ELLIE ENJOY SINGING SUNDAY SCHOOL SONGS. "Jesus Loves Me" is their favorite. They like to sing, "Jesus loves me, this I know. For the Bible tells me so."

The Bible tells us that when Jesus lived on earth, He spent time with children. He loved them. Even when big crowds came to see Jesus, He said, "Let the little children come to me."

Jesus loves children today just as much as He did back then. He lives in heaven now, but just like God, Jesus sees you and He knows all about you. He loves you with all His heart. Jesus loves every boy and girl wherever they live in the world.

Sophia and Ellie show Jesus they love Him by singing, sharing with each other, and being helpful. Can you think of other ways to show Jesus you love Him?

I am blessed because Jesus loves me
and God knows my name.

God Knows Your Name

"I have called you by name, and you are mine."
ISAIAH 43:1

LONG AGO, SHEPHERD BOYS CARED FOR BIG FLOCKS OF SHEEP. It was their job to take the sheep to pastures where they could eat. Every morning, the shepherds called their sheep by name. "Hurry up, Dexter. Get a move on, Sadie. Good boy, Alexander." There were so many names to remember, but the shepherds knew them all.

God cares for people like a good shepherd. He knows the names of everyone on earth. Can you imagine knowing everybody's name? And God never forgets a name. He made everyone, and He knows exactly who they are. When God looks down from heaven and sees you, He doesn't say, "Look at that kid over there." He calls you by name.

Count how many times you hear your name today. Whenever you hear it, remember that God knows your name and He loves you.

9

You Are One of a Kind

I praise you because you made me in an
amazing and wonderful way.
PSALM 139:14

THERE IS NOBODY IN THE WHOLE WORLD EXACTLY LIKE YOU.
God made you extra special. Even if you were a twin, you would be
different from everyone else.

God blesses each person with differences. It might be the way
you look, but it can also be the way you talk and act or the things
you like and believe in.

Did you know that you are a little bit like a snowflake? God made
no two snowflakes exactly alike, just like no two people are exactly
the same. There is only one you, and there will never be someone
just like you. God made you one of a kind!

*Think about your best friend. In what ways
are you alike? How are you different?*

Jesus is the greatest
blessing of all.

The Most Amazing Baby

Today your Savior was born in David's town. He is Christ, the Lord.

LUKE 2:11

JESUS CAME INTO THE WORLD AS A NEWBORN BABY. His mother, Mary, and her husband, Joseph, had traveled from a faraway place to a town called Bethlehem. When they arrived, there was no place for them to stay. So Mary and Joseph went to a stable to rest. There, in the middle of the night, baby Jesus was born.

Shepherds were in the fields caring for their sheep when, suddenly, angels appeared to them in a great, white light. They told the shepherds that a very special baby had just been born—a baby who, when He grew up, would do something amazing. This amazing thing would save people from dying! The shepherds hurried to Bethlehem to see this special boy.

Another name for Jesus is "Christ." We call His birthday Christmas.

11

Look What You Can Do!

For we are God's masterpiece.

EPHESIANS 2:10 NLT

TARA LIKES TO DANCE. Do you? She loves swirling and twirling as she moves to the music.

Your body can move in many wonderful ways. When you were a tiny baby, you could blink your eyes and wiggle your fingers and toes. As you grew, you learned to wave, walk, run, and jump. Your body does so many amazing things that you can't count them all.

The Bible says we are God's masterpiece. A masterpiece is someone's best work of art. That's you—God's best work! He created your body to do all kinds of things. You can use it to climb, kick a ball, draw, and even dance like Tara.

Use your body to help someone today. Use your hands to set the table and put your toys away. What other things can you do?

Blessings That Taste Good

Here is a boy with five loaves of barley bread and two little fish. But that is not enough for so many people.

JOHN 6:9

WHEN JESUS GREW UP, PEOPLE WANTED TO HEAR HIM TALK ABOUT LIVING RIGHT AND PLEASING GOD. Big crowds followed Him wherever He went.

One day, five thousand people spent the whole day listening to Jesus. By evening, they were all very hungry. The only food was a young boy's lunch—five small loaves of bread and two little fish. Jesus took the lunch and thanked God for it. Then Jesus did something amazing. A miracle! Jesus made the bread and fish turn into enough food to feed *all* those people! And oh, it tasted so good.

Isn't it special that God blesses people with good, tasty food and mouths to eat it?

 What do you like to eat? What tastes good to you?

Thank You for hands and feet to run and play and for yummy food to eat!

Joy, Joy, Joy

Always be joyful.
1 THESSALONIANS 5:16 NIRV

WHEN ETHAN WOKE UP, HE SMELLED PANCAKES COOKING. He hurried to the kitchen, where his mother was making breakfast.

"Pancakes!" said Ethan. "Pancakes make me happy!"

After breakfast, Ethan still felt joyful. He ran around the living room, flapping his arms, pretending to be a bird.

"Pretending makes me happy!" he said.

He hopped down the hall to his bedroom, put on his clothes, and went outside to play.

Ethan ran with his puppy and swung on his swing. He played with his trucks.

"Playing makes me joyful!" he said.

So many things made Ethan feel happy.

Did you know that God wants you to be joyful too? When He fills up your heart with joy, it is His way of saying, "I love you."

 What made you joyful today? What can you do to help someone else feel joyful?

Thank You, Lord, for putting joy in my heart.

God's Perfect Son

"For God loved the world so much
that he gave his only Son."

JOHN 3:16

GOD HAS A SON NAMED JESUS. Maybe you have heard of Him.
God cares so much about people that He sent Jesus down to earth
to live with them for a while.

There are many stories about Jesus in the Bible. He was kind
and gentle, and everything He did was right and true. He showed
people what God is like and how to live a life that pleases Him. And
here's the best part—Jesus is God's most wonderful blessing. Do
you know why? Because Jesus made it possible for everyone to live
in heaven someday. Jesus is the greatest person who ever lived.

*Fold your hands, bow your head, and say this little
prayer: "Thank You, God, for giving us Jesus. Amen."*

15

I Think . . .

You have known the Holy Scriptures since you were a child. The Scriptures are able to make you wise.

2 TIMOTHY 3:15

YOUR BRAIN IS ANOTHER OF THOSE EVERYDAY BLESSINGS. Think about it. If God had not blessed you with a brain, you could not think at all.

Your brain fits nicely inside your head. Still, it has enough space to store a whole lifetime of thinking. Everything you learn is stored there. Your brain also tells your other body parts what to do.

You get to choose much of what you put inside your brain. The best thing you can put in there is God's Word—the Bible. The Bible is filled with God's wisdom. When you read the Bible, your brain stores up all that wisdom. At times when you need to make choices, God's wisdom will be there to help you.

Make a fist with both hands and then put your hands together. Your brain is about that big!

God's Greatest Blessing

"He who believes in me will have life even if he dies."
JOHN 11:25

SOME PEOPLE DIDN'T LIKE JESUS. They didn't believe that He was good and God's perfect Son. So they arrested Jesus. They nailed His hands and feet to a big wooden cross and left Him there to die.

But God did something. It seemed terrible at first, but it would be God's greatest blessing. He filled Jesus' heart with every naughty thing people had ever done and would ever do. Jesus loved us so much that He took the blame for it all. He hurt and died for us so that anyone who believes in what He did and asks God for forgiveness can live in heaven with God forever.

⭐ *Did you know that naughty things have no place in heaven? Everything there is perfect. Jesus took the blame for every naughty thing we do so when we die, we can live in heaven with Him.*

I am grateful for a mind to think and a heart to love Jesus.

Amazing Things

He has done great and wonderful things for you.
You have seen them with your own eyes.

DEUTERONOMY 10:21

SOME OF GOD'S BLESSINGS ARE SO AMAZING THAT YOU CANNOT MISS THEM. He made mountains called volcanoes that spit smoke and fire into the sky. He made geysers—boiling streams under the earth that send tall sprays of hot water up from the ground and into the air. Sometimes God allows the earth to shake and huge waves to roll across the ocean. Long ago, He created a deep, rocky hole in the earth called the Grand Canyon. People still come from all over the world to see it. Once in a while, God lets the moon block the sun's light. Then, for a few minutes, daytime looks like night.

This all-powerful God, who does such amazing things, loves you! That is His best blessing of all.

Say this little prayer: "Thank You, God, for being so great. Thank You, God, for loving me. Amen."

My Heavenly Father

We are God's children.

ROMANS 8:16

WHEN YOU BELIEVE THAT JESUS DIED AND TOOK THE BLAME FOR THE NAUGHTY THINGS WE ALL DO, YOU BECOME A CHILD OF GOD.

God is called the heavenly Father. He watches over all His children, and He loves them and gives them blessings. God stays with His children all the time. He never leaves them alone.

You can talk with God, your heavenly Father, whenever you want. All you have to do is pray. When you pray, you are talking to God, and He will hear you. You can tell Him anything. God is the kind of Father who loves hearing from His children. He wants you to tell Him about your feelings and ask Him for whatever you need.

Say this little prayer: "Dear heavenly Father, thank You for watching over me and loving me. I love You too. Amen."

Thank You, God, for being my Father.

He Lives!

Jesus is not here. He has risen from death!
LUKE 24:6

GOD WASN'T DONE YET. Three days after Jesus died, God brought Him back to life. Jesus came back to prove God's promise that after our bodies die, we can still live forever. And that's just what Jesus did! After coming back for a little while, He went up to heaven, and He lives there right now with God.

Today when people die, their bodies don't come back to life like Jesus' did. He was very special. But if you believe in what He did, then someday you too can live forever in heaven. Jesus proved it by showing Himself to people after He died and rose again.

⭐ *God loves you so much*
that He blessed you now with a body
to live in here on earth and later
with a special place in heaven.

God has blessed us with the promise of heaven—a home with the King of kings.

The Greatest King

He is the King of all kings and the Lord of all lords.

1 TIMOTHY 6:15

ONCE UPON A TIME, THERE WAS A GREAT KING . . . Do you know stories that begin that way?

There are stories about great kings who do great things and bad kings who do evil things, stories about mixed-up kings, silly kings, old kings, and even little boy kings. There are hundreds of stories about kings. But do you know who is the greatest King of all?

God!

God is not like the kings in stories. The Bible calls Him King of kings because He is greater than any king who has ever lived or ever will. God is the King of Everything. He rules over the world and its people. He blesses with goodness those who love Him.

Can you imagine God sitting on His throne in heaven?

 *If you were a king, what kind of king would you be? Why?*

God's Special Helper

But the Lord's Spirit has filled me
with power and strength.

MICAH 3:8

ALONG WITH JESUS, GOD BLESSED THE WORLD WITH SOMEONE ELSE. He is called the Holy Spirit, and like Jesus, He is a part of God.

It is the Holy Spirit's job to help you feel God's love and also to help you love God back. You can't see the Holy Spirit, but you can feel Him in your heart. When you are about to do something naughty and a little voice inside you says, "You'd better not," that's the Holy Spirit. He gives you the power to do what is right. He also fills your heart with God's love. The Holy Spirit reminds you of Jesus and the wonderful things He did and said.

Because the Holy Spirit is invisible and doesn't have a body, God can send Him anywhere. Do you know where He lives? Inside your heart!

God has blessed us with the Holy Spirit to comfort and guide us.

Counting Stars

He counts the stars and names each one.
PSALM 147:4

JOSIE AND HER DADDY LIKE LOOKING AT THE NIGHT SKY. Through their telescope, they see planets, the moon, and stars. Josie wants to count all the stars, but there are too many. Her daddy says that there are more stars than any human can see. Some are so far away that you can't even see them with a telescope.

No person can count all the stars. The only One who can is God. He knows exactly how many stars there are because He made them all.

The Bible says that God gave each star a name. If you could name a star, what would you call it?

Go outside with a parent at night, and look at the sky. How many stars do you guess are up there? The moon and stars are amazing blessings—gifts to you from God.

What Do You Hear?

The Lord has made both these things: Ears
that can hear and eyes that can see.

PROVERBS 20:12

ONE WINTER NIGHT, ELIZABETH AND HER DADDY WENT FOR
A WALK. The world was so still that you could almost hear the
snowflakes fall.

Who-who-who. Who-who . . .

"What was that?" Elizabeth said.

Who-who-who. Who-who . . .

Just then, the sound of great whooshing wings swept through
the air, and a snowy owl landed on a nearby tree branch.

"Look, Daddy!" said Elizabeth. "That's what made the sound."

God put all kinds of sounds in the world for you to hear. Listen
and you just might hear an owl, like Elizabeth did. Or you might
hear a distant train whistle or a dog barking. God blessed you with
ears to hear. So listen. What do you hear?

*Sit quietly now, and use your ears. Can
you hear yourself breathing?
Thank You, God, for ears
that hear!*

God's Bedtime Promise

You won't need to be afraid when you lie down.
When you lie down, your sleep will be peaceful.
PROVERBS 3:24

WHEN DIEGO'S MOMMY TUCKED HIM IN, DIEGO SAID, "CHECK THE CLOSET AND UNDER THE BED." He wanted his mommy to make sure that everything in his room was safe and sound. "And please leave the light on," Diego said. He did not like sleeping in the dark.

If Diego had thought about God's promises, he might not have felt afraid. God, the great King of Everything, promises to bless His children with peaceful sleep. He promises to love them and stay with them, in their room, all night long. There was nothing in Diego's room that God did not know about and nothing that God could not take care of.

Do you know someone who is afraid of the dark? You can help by telling that person about God's promises. Do you remember what they are?

I am thankful God watches over me through the night.

I Love God Back

We should worship God in a way that pleases him.
HEBREWS 12:28

WORSHIP IS A WORD THAT MEANS SHOWING GOD YOU LOVE HIM. Worship is more than just going to church and Sunday school. It is spending time with God, obeying Him, and appreciating all that He does.

Becca loves God. She worships Him when she prays by thanking Him for His blessings. She also tells God how great and wonderful He is. Sometimes Becca sings songs to God and dances a happy dance.

Loving God fills Becca's heart with joy. The Bible says to worship God joyfully. So Becca shows God how much she loves Him by worshipping Him with joyful words and songs.

You can worship God too. Tell God right now that you love Him. Tell Him how great you think He is, and thank Him for all His blessings. If you want to, you can sing Him a happy song.

My heart is filled with the blessing of God's love.

God Loves Me Forever

"I love you people with a love that will last forever."
JEREMIAH 31:3

GOD HAS A SPECIAL PROMISE FOR YOU. He promises to love you. Not just sometimes, not just when you are being good, but forever. Forever is a long, long time. Forever has no beginning and no end. Forever is all the time and always.

God thought you up. He made you, and you were in His care even before you were born. He didn't make you by accident. God made you on purpose, and He made you so that He could love you. No matter what you do, God never stops loving you. His love for you is a gift—a blessing!

Try to think about God all the time. The more you think about Him, the more you will remember that He loves you.

Draw a picture of a big heart. Print on it the words "God loves me."

27

A Rainbow Promise

"I am putting my rainbow in the clouds. It is the sign of the agreement between me and the earth."

GENESIS 9:13

LONG AGO, THERE WAS SO MUCH SIN IN THE WORLD THAT GOD PLANNED A DO-OVER. He planned to wash all the sin away in a flood that would cover up the earth.

God told His friend Noah to build a giant boat. "Put two of every kind of animal inside," said God.

Saggy, baggy elephants; tall, spotted giraffes; tiny mice; roaring lions; squawking chickens—they all marched in. Then Noah shut the door.

Whoosh! The big flood came and covered the earth. But Noah, his family, and all the animals were safe.

After God had cleaned the world of all the sinful people, He put a rainbow in the sky. "This is My promise," He said. "I will never again cover up the whole world with water."

God still blesses the world with rainbows. The next time you see one, you can remember the big cleanup flood and that God loves you.

More Promises

*I am as happy over your promises as if
I had found a great treasure.*

PSALM 119:162

GOD HAS MADE MANY WONDERFUL PROMISES TO HIS
CHILDREN. When He promised to send Someone to rescue them
from all the sin in the world, He sent Jesus. Through Jesus, God
promised a place in heaven for everyone who believes.

God promises to help you when you are in trouble and to give
you rest when you are tired. He promises to make you strong when
you need to be and to teach you to be good. He promises to listen
to you, give you exactly what you need, and always love you.

God has many more promises ready for you in the Bible. As you
grow older and learn more about Him, you will discover more of His
promise-blessings. Each one is like finding a treasure.

 *Make a promise today. Promise to pray
for someone or to help that friend.*

**God has filled the Bible
with blessings and promises!**

Friendship

A friend loves you all the time.

PROVERBS 17:17

"HEY, LUCAS," SAID NICK. "Come to the fair with us this Saturday."

"I can't," Lucas said. "I'm going to the fair with my cousins."

Nick felt disappointed. He did everything with Lucas, and he really wanted to go to the fair with his friend. Nick felt a little angry that Lucas couldn't go. But then he remembered some words from the Bible: "A friend loves you all the time." That's the kind of friend that God wants you to be, a friend who loves and is slow to get angry.

"That's okay, Lucas," said Nick. "We can have fun another day."

God blessed Nick with a good friend, and Nick knows the best way to keep Lucas's friendship is to love him all the time. Love means treating your friends the way Jesus would.

Did Nick do the right thing? What would you say if your friend couldn't do what you wanted to do?

God, please help me to be a good friend and to keep my promises so I can bless others.

God, the Promise Keeper

God is not a man. He will not lie. God is not a
human being. He does not change his mind.

NUMBERS 23:19

JACK WAS BUSY BUILDING SOMETHING GRAND.

"Will you play with your little sister?" asked his mother.

"In a minute," said Jack. "I promise."

But Jack got so busy with building that he forgot about his
promise. People do that sometimes. They don't mean to break
promises, but they forget or maybe they change their minds.

God is not like people. Everything He says is true because God
does not lie and He does not change His mind. You can always
count on God, the Promise Keeper, not only to keep His promises,
but also to help you to keep yours.

When Jack remembered his promise, he invited his sister to play
with him, and together they built something grand.

When you break a promise, what should you say?
"I'm sorry. Please forgive me!"

Grandparent Blessings

Gray hair is like a crown of honor. You
earn it by living a good life.

PROVERBS 16:31

GRANDPARENTS ARE A SPECIAL BLESSING. One of the most
important things about grandparents is that they are very wise.
They have lived a long time and have learned many things.
Grandparents can teach you about almost anything.

Eli's grandma is a good storyteller. She likes telling Eli true
stories about people in the Bible. Eli's grandma told him about
a man named Paul who traveled far and near telling people all
about Jesus. On one of his journeys, Paul met a young man named
Timothy. When Timothy was little, his grandmother liked telling
him Bible stories too. Because Timothy learned about God from his
grandmother, he grew up loving God, and he became one of Paul's
best helpers. Together, Paul and Timothy told the world about God's
amazing love.

*Can you think of some other ways that
grandparents are blessings?*

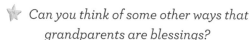

Grandparents are
a wonderful gift from God.

Cousin John

This is the voice of a man who calls out:
"Prepare in the desert the way for the Lord."
ISAIAH 40:3

DO YOU HAVE COUSINS? Jesus did. He had a cousin named John. People called him John the Baptist. God gave John a very special purpose. It was John's job to go on ahead of Jesus and say, "Get ready. Jesus is coming!" John baptized people by putting water on them in a river. Baptism shows that a person wants to live a clean life and be a child of God.

God blesses everyone with a purpose. You might not know what your purpose is, but you can know that God sends everybody into the world for His own special reason. If you believe in and trust God, then He will use you to help with His plans.

⭐ *John the Baptist lived in the wilderness. He wore clothes made from camel's hair, and he ate grasshoppers and honey! Draw a picture of him.*

A Room in God's House

"There are many rooms in my Father's house. I would not tell you this if it were not true. I am going there to prepare a place for you."

JOHN 14:2

THINK ABOUT WHERE YOU LIVE. Is your house in a neighborhood with many other houses? Maybe you live in an apartment building, or on a farm, or in a mobile home. God blesses His children with places to live. Each house has different rooms used for different things, a kitchen, bathroom, living room, bedroom . . . How many rooms are in your house? Did you know some people don't have a home at all? God wants us to pray for them and find ways to help them.

Jesus told about God's house in heaven. He said that it has many rooms. There are so many rooms that God has a place for every person who will live there someday. God will have a place waiting for you when you get to heaven too! Jesus has gone on ahead of you to get it ready.

What would you like your room in God's house to look like?

34

I Can Lead

Don't let anyone look down on you because you are young, but set an example for the believers in speech, in conduct, in love, in faith and in purity.

1 TIMOTHY 4:12 NIV

GROWN-UPS ARE NOT THE ONLY LEADERS. Kids can lead too.

Joey is a good leader. He is the oldest kid in his family. His younger brothers and sisters look up to him. They want to be just like Joey someday. Joey is a leader because he sets a good example. He never says mean things or uses bad words. He acts with love toward his brothers and sisters. He helps teach them right from wrong. And when he messes up, Joey asks for forgiveness. Joey's leadership is a blessing to his family. Joey thinks a lot about how Jesus treated others, and he tries to be like Him.

You can be a leader too. You can start by setting a good example for your family and friends.

 Name three ways that you can set a good example.

Lord, please help my example to be a blessing to others.

Family Blessings

"My true brother and sister and mother are
those who do the things God wants."

MARK 3:35

ONE OF GOD'S MOST WONDERFUL BLESSINGS IS YOUR FAMILY—
THE PEOPLE WHO LOVE YOU. God made your family, and He made
you a part of it. Families come in all sizes, big, little, and everything
in between. What size is yours?

Did you know that you are part of another family? As a child of
God, you belong to His family too. God's family is huge. It includes
everyone who loves Him: children, moms, dads, grandmas, grandpas,
aunts, uncles, cousins . . . God is the Father of them all. God loves
every member of His family more than anyone ever could. He is
always there for them no matter what. God not only loves everyone in
His family, but He loves everyone in your family too.

*Make a list of all your family members.
How many names are on your list?*

Best Friends

"You are my friends if you do what I command you."
JOHN 15:14

THERE ARE FRIENDS ALL AROUND YOU, IN YOUR NEIGHBOR-
HOOD, AT CHURCH, AT SCHOOL. Everywhere!

Jesus is your friend too, and He is a very special blessing to you
from God. Jesus is your *best* Friend. He loves you so much that
He died for your sins. He went to heaven to make a place for you
someday. You can trust Jesus with anything. He is always with you
to listen to your prayers and to help with whatever you need. Jesus
will never leave you. Wherever you go and whatever you do, He will
be there forever. Now, that's a great friend!

What kind of friend are you to Jesus? Do you spend time talking
with Him in prayer? Have you told your friends about Him?

⭐ *Name some ways that Jesus is a blessing to you.
Remember to thank Him for being your friend.*

I am blessed by
my friend Jesus.

My Neighborhood

Then the Lord God said, "It is not good
for the man to be alone."

GENESIS 2:18

GOD SAID IT ISN'T GOOD TO BE ALONE. In the beginning, He didn't make just one animal; He made many. And when God created the first man, Adam, He made Eve to be Adam's helper. God puts us in groups because He knows that it is good.

The people who live near you are your neighbors. Think about your neighborhood, the people who live across the street, next door, upstairs, downstairs, around the block . . . God made them all. He put you together in a neighborhood with other people because it is not good to be alone. Good neighbors are a blessing. They watch out for each other and help keep the neighborhood safe.

How do the people in your neighborhood help each other? What can you do to help your neighbors?

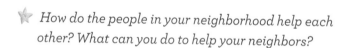

I want to be a blessing
to my neighbors.

38

The Golden Rule

"Treat others as you want them to treat you."
MATTHEW 7:12 CEV

GOD MADE US ALL, AND HE PUT US TOGETHER ON EARTH. You can think of earth as one big neighborhood, and everyone who lives here is your neighbor.

Being a good neighbor is so important to God that He made a rule about it. The Golden Rule says, "Love your neighbor." That means God wants you to treat everybody in the world just like you want to be treated. The Golden Rule is God's love in action. It is a blessing because when you obey it, the world becomes a better place.

You can love your neighbors by being helpful and kind without expecting anything in return. You can pray for your neighbors too. Prayer is a great way to love them.

Ask a parent to help you make a plan to help a neighbor. What can you do to be helpful and kind?

39

Heavenly Blessings

How awesome is this place! This is none
other than the house of God.

GENESIS 28:17 NIV

HEAVEN IS A BEAUTIFUL PLACE. It is so beautiful that no pictures or words can describe it. Heaven is God's house. He rules it as the King of kings. He sits in heaven on His throne with Jesus sitting next to Him.

Heaven is filled with wonderful blessings that nobody living on earth has ever felt or seen. Angels in heaven worship God with songs and music, and the whole place brims with light and love that come from God Himself. Everything in heaven is perfect.

God loves you so much that He sent Jesus to make a way for you to get to heaven one day. To get there, you need to trust Jesus and believe that He died for your sins.

Say this little prayer: "Thank You, God, for saving a place for me in heaven. Amen."

Everything You Need

My God will use his wonderful riches in Christ
Jesus to give you everything you need.

PHILIPPIANS 4:19

LOOK AROUND THE NEAREST CITY OR TOWN, AND YOU WILL
SEE ALL KINDS OF BLESSINGS. There are stores to shop in, schools
to learn in, fire stations, hospitals, movie theaters, churches, and
plenty of places to have fun with your friends. Cars and buses will
take you wherever you want to go. Whatever you need is nearby:
food, water, fun, and plenty of helpers.

God planned ahead to bless you with the things you need. And
He knows that nothing happens unless people have neighbors who
work together to help each other. Helping one another and being
a good neighbor makes a city or town work—and that includes
blessing our neighbors in need.

*Think about the city you live in. What favorite places
has God blessed you with? What is your favorite place
to have fun? Where is your favorite place to eat?*

Heaven is filled with wonderful blessings—
better than anything we can imagine.

41

Community Helpers

My help comes from the Lord. He made heaven and earth.

PSALM 121:2

MRS. CRUZ WAITED FOR MIA AND HER BROTHER AT THE STREET CORNER. "Look both ways," she said. "Here we go." Mrs. Cruz blew her whistle. She walked into the middle of the street and held up her stop sign. Mia and her brother crossed the street safely. "See you tomorrow," Mrs. Cruz said.

Mia told her daddy, "I love Mrs. Cruz. She's the best crossing guard in the whole world! And she's nice too."

Crossing guards are a blessing. They help children stay safe when crossing the street.

God blesses communities with all kinds of helpers. Look around. Helpers are everywhere! Police officers, firefighters, bus drivers, teachers, doctors, nurses, pastors, clerks in stores . . . Can you think of others?

 Choose one person you think is a special helper. Make a thank-you card to give that person.

Helpers can bless people all over the world!

Friends Around the World

Do your best to live in peace with everyone.
ROMANS 12:18

MICHAEL'S SUNDAY SCHOOL CLASS SENT PICTURES OF THEMSELVES AND LETTERS TO A SUNDAY SCHOOL CLASS IN AFRICA. The children in Africa sent letters and pictures back to Michael's class.

God blesses people with different places to live, and that makes life interesting. Learning about other places and people is fun. Michael's class discovered how children live in Africa. The children in Africa learned about life in America. Although the children lived far from each other, they became good friends. The world is God's big neighborhood, and He wants everyone to get along.

The Bible tells us to do our best to live at peace with everyone. One way to do that is to make friends around the world.

⭐ *Ask your mom and dad where their relatives came from. Do you know someone who lives in another part of the world?*

43

My Country

Happy is the nation whose God is the Lord.

PSALM 33:12

THE WORLD IS A VERY BIG PLACE. Its land is divided into areas called countries. Kids live in countries all around the world. Anthony lives in the United States. Luca lives in Germany. Maria lives in Mexico, and Riko lives in Japan.

What country do you live in?

Each country has its own special ways of doing things. The people in different countries speak different languages. They celebrate holidays in different ways. People have different ideas about many things. Some people believe in God and some do not.

Your country is a gift from God—a blessing. God wants people in all of the world's countries to believe in Him. The Bible says that believing in God brings a country happiness.

Say a prayer today for people who don't believe in God. Ask God to help them believe.

Good leaders can be great blessings.

Leaders

Doing what is right makes a nation great.
PROVERBS 14:34

LONG AGO, GOD ASKED A MAN NAMED MOSES TO LEAD HIS PEOPLE OUT OF A BAD COUNTRY AND INTO A GOOD ONE. Moses listened to God. He tried his best to do exactly what God said. Moses was a good leader. He knew that following God and doing what was right would make his country great.

God blesses the world with leaders. They lead your church, your community, and your country. A Sunday school teacher is a leader. She leads the class and teaches them about Jesus. The mayor of a city is a leader. He leads a community. The president of the United States is a leader too. He leads a big country. Leaders are trusted with the power to get things done. A good leader does what is fair and right.

Do you know a good leader? What can you do to thank him or her?

All-Powerful God

But God has wisdom and power. He has
good advice and understanding.

JOB 12:13

DO YOU KNOW WHO IS THE MOST POWERFUL LEADER? God!
God is more powerful than any king, queen, or president who has
ever lived. God rules the world. He rules everyone and everything
with love.

God is the greatest Leader because He always does what is fair
and right. Always. God never makes mistakes. He is very wise, and
He makes perfect decisions. God has the power to do anything.
There is nothing that He cannot do. God is the Leader of all leaders.
He gives good advice. Best of all, God understands. He knows
better than anyone what is going on in the world. Good leaders
know that they should trust God with everything they do.

 Make a poster for your room with the words "Trust God."

I am thankful that
God is powerful and fair.

Be Fair

You bless those people who are honest
and fair in everything they do.
PSALM 106:3 CEV

"THAT'S NOT FAIR!" COLTON SAID. "Mom, Ben took the last cookie
and you said that I could have it."

Ben looked guilty. He knew he had done something wrong. That
cookie belonged to his little brother, but Ben ate it anyway. What
Ben did was not fair. Fairness means being honest and following
the rules.

God is the fairest One of all. Everything God does is honest. He
doesn't have to worry about following the rules because He makes
all the rules. God expects fairness from everyone, especially people
who lead. Ben could have been a good leader and done what is right.
He could have set a good example for his younger brother.

*If you were Ben, would you have eaten the cookie? The Bible
says that God blesses people who are fair in everything they do.*

God Leads Me

He leads me on paths that are right.
PSALM 23:3

FOLLOW THE LEADER IS A FUN GAME. When you play, you follow your friends and do everything they do. But sometimes following is not a good idea. You would not follow a leader who leads you into a busy street, would you? A good leader leads followers along a safe path, even when playing a game.

God is that kind of leader. He blesses people by knowing exactly where everyone is going. If people trust Him, He will always lead them in the right way. When people don't trust God, they sometimes get lost. They go in a way that leads to trouble.

The best way to follow God is to find out all you can about Jesus. He loves you. He knows which way is right, and He will always lead you in the right direction.

Play Follow the Leader with your friends. Lead them where it is safe.

Blessings That Smell Good

*If the whole body were an eye, the body would
not be able to hear. If the whole body were an ear,
the body would not be able to smell anything.*

1 CORINTHIANS 12:17

WHAT SMELLS DO YOU IMAGINE WHEN YOU THINK OF
THANKSGIVING? Turkey? Cranberries? What about Christmas?
The sweet smell of cookies baking? The fresh smell of Christmas
trees? The spicy smell of peppermint candy?

Along with eyes to see and ears to hear, God blessed people with
noses to smell.

Different places and things have different smells. Christmas
in the stable where Jesus was born smelled very different from
Christmas at your house. The smell of fresh hay was all around and
also the smell of dusty, woolly sheep. The night smelled new. And
when three wise men came to see Jesus, they brought perfumes
called frankincense and myrrh that made the air smell wonderful.

 *What things does your nose like to smell?*

**Thank You, God,
for good-smelling things.**

Spread the Love

"This is my command: Love each other as I have loved you."
JOHN 15:12

THERE ARE LITTLE WAYS THAT YOU CAN HELP SPREAD GOD'S LOVE AROUND.

Gavin's mom is very busy. When she comes home from work, she feels tired. She cannot rest until everything gets done. Gavin spreads God's love around by helping his mom. He picks up his toys and keeps his room neat. He also helps set the table and take out the trash. Helping his mom gives her more time to spend with Gavin.

Zoe is a helper too. She spreads God's love by taking good care of her pets. She makes sure that they have fresh food and water and that their cages are clean.

When you spread God's love around, you help Him bless others. Sometimes helping in small ways is the best blessing of all.

⭐ *What things can you do to help out at home?*

A Giving Spirit

The good person gives without holding back.
PROVERBS 21:26

HAVE YOU EVER GIVEN AWAY SOMETHING THAT YOU WANTED TO KEEP? God did. He loves people so much that He gave up His one and only Son, Jesus. He sent Jesus into the world to take the punishment for all the bad things people do. If God had not done that, then nobody would ever get to heaven. God loves us so much that He gave the world the One He loved most.

That is how God is, always giving to us. Every one of His gifts is a blessing. He blesses us because He loves us more than anything else.

God wants people to be givers too. When people give time, money, food, or anything else to those who need, they help to spread God's love around. Giving to others is a blessing.

 Can you name someone who has given you something?

It is a blessing to spread God's love and give to others.

Cheerful Givers

God loves the person who gives happily.
2 CORINTHIANS 9:7

HAILEY WAS SO EXCITED! She and her mom had made a gift basket full of delicious treats for their sick neighbor, Mrs. Ellsworth.

"Oh, come in!" Mrs. Ellsworth said. "Come in and visit with me for a while."

Hailey and her mom spent the morning with their neighbor. They shared the treats and talked. They offered to run errands and to help clean Mrs. Ellsworth's house.

"This is such a blessing," said Mrs. Ellsworth. "You are such generous and kind neighbors."

It made Hailey feel happy to spend time with her neighbor and to share her gifts.

The Bible tells us that God loves a cheerful giver. That is the kind of giver God is. When He does something nice for you, it makes Him happy. God loves giving good things to you because He loves you so much!

 Draw a picture of a cheerful giver.

Thank You for blessing me with special gifts!

Special Gifts

We all have different gifts. Each gift came
because of the grace that God gave us.

ROMANS 12:6

WHEN GOD MADE YOU ONE OF A KIND, HE GAVE YOU CERTAIN
THINGS THAT YOU DO WELL. Those things are called skills, or
talents. Maybe you can sing well or dance. Maybe you are a good
listener. You might be good at art and crafts, or maybe you give
great instructions and help others learn new things.

Jesus is an example of someone with many skills. He
was a perfect leader. He was good at listening to people and
understanding their needs. And Jesus was really good with sick
people. He knew just what to do to make them well.

Skills are blessings from God. He knew, even before you were
born, what special skills you would have. He blessed you with those
skills so He can use you to bless others.

*Name three things you are good at. How
can you use those things to bless others?*

Good News!

How beautiful on the mountains are the
feet of those who bring good news.

ISAIAH 52:7 NIV

AKIN AND HIS DADDY WENT TO THE BEACH. "Follow me, Akin," Daddy said. Their feet took them near the water. Wet sand squished between their toes. Their feet made footprints wherever they went.

When God made people, He knew that they needed feet to do special things. So God blessed them with feet that could kick balls, ride bikes, climb trees, jump high, run up a big hill, and take them wherever they wanted to go. Best of all, feet take people all over the world to spread the Good News about Jesus—that He died so someday we can live forever in heaven with God.

Use your feet today. Go tell someone about Jesus. You could tell your mommy or daddy, a brother or sister, or a friend.

I am grateful I can share the Good News.
It's the *best* news!

Teamwork!

Two people are better than one. They get more done by working together.

ECCLESIASTES 4:9

CHAD PLAYS SOCCER ON A TEAM WITH OTHER BOYS AND GIRLS. He is learning about teamwork. When he and his team work together, they score more points.

Jesus believed in teamwork. He chose twelve men as His helpers. Together, Jesus and His friends worked to tell people about God.

God loves it when people work together in teams. He knows that when people put their special skills together, they can do great things. A team working together can help God bless others. Teams can pack up care boxes to send to soldiers or collect food for people who need it. A team working together can spread God's blessings all around the world.

⭐ *Think of some ways that you and your family can work together in your community to spread God's love.*

Kindness Everywhere

When we have the opportunity to help anyone, we should do it.

GALATIANS 6:10

GOD LOVES YOU WITH KINDNESS. Do you notice all the kind little things He does for you? He blesses you with food to eat, clothes to wear, and a place to live. He puts things around you to make you laugh and smile.

Being kind to others is a way to share God's love. Often kindness is shown in small ways. You can hold the door open for someone or let him go first in line. You can invite a new friend for a play date. You can say, "Hello," "Thank you," and, "Good morning." You can smile! You can make something for someone or say something nice about how she looks or what she did. When you think about it, you can find all sorts of ways to spread around God's love.

 How can you be kind to an animal? A friend? Your family?

God, please help me to bless the world with kindness.

Caring for the Earth

The Lord God put the man in the garden
of Eden to care for it and work it.

GENESIS 2:15

EMILY'S BROTHER TOSSED A PLASTIC WATER BOTTLE INTO THE TRASH.

"Wait a minute!" said Emily. "We should recycle that."

Emily knows that it is important to care for the earth. One way she helps is by keeping reusable things from going into the trash.

When God made the earth, He filled it with beautiful things for people to enjoy. The earth is His blessing. It is the home that God made for people to live in. After He made it, God put people in charge of the earth, and He expects them to take good care of it.

You can help care for God's earth by not wasting anything and by picking up your trash. With a grown-up's permission, you can make the earth prettier by planting flowers or a tree.

 Can you think of other ways to care for God's earth?

Quiet Giving

"Your giving should be done in secret."

MATTHEW 6:4

WHAT IF EVERY TIME GOD BLESSED SOMEONE, HE SHOUTED FROM HEAVEN IN A BIG, BOOMING VOICE, "LOOK WHAT I DID! I BLESSED ERIC (OR KARA, OR AUNT LUCY, OR GRANDPA JIM)!" Why, the whole world would stop and take notice.

When God blesses people, He does it quietly. His blessings are sometimes like hidden treasures. You won't see them unless you look hard. And when you find one, you feel His love.

God expects you to give quietly too. When you give to someone, it should be because you love that person, not because you want attention.

Secret gifts are the quietest of all. When you give a secret gift, you tell no one, not even your best friend. Only you and God know. Secret gifts bless people and keep them guessing about the giver.

Do something special for someone today.
Keep it a secret between you and God.

Give God Some Love

*Love the Lord your God with all your
heart, soul and strength.*

DEUTERONOMY 6:5

GOD ALWAYS BLESSES YOU WITH HIS LOVE. So shouldn't you love Him back?

There are many ways to show God you love Him. You can love Him by behaving and by helping others. You can also show your love to God by worshipping Him and going to church.

Sari tells God she loves Him every night when she says her prayers. At Sunday school she shows God her love by paying attention to her teacher. She sings songs in Sunday school to worship God, and when she attends church with her parents, she sits quietly until the service ends. The best way Sari gives her love to God is by telling others about Him. Sari is always noticing God's blessings and sharing them with her friends.

When you think about God's blessings, you will find it easy to love Him.

 Can you name and count your blessings?

Secret gifts—surprise gifts!—
are special blessings.

Be Generous

*A person who gives to others will get richer.
Whoever helps others will himself be helped.*

PROVERBS 11:25

DYLAN'S MOM CLEANED OUT HIS CLOSET AND DECIDED TO GIVE AWAY SOME OF HIS OLD CLOTHES.

"I don't want to give that shirt away!" Dylan said. "I like that shirt."

"But it doesn't fit you anymore," said his mother.

"I don't care," Dylan said. "It's mine, and I want to keep it."

Then Dylan remembered something he had learned in Sunday school: when you give to someone, it is like giving to God. That made Dylan want to give his shirt away. God had blessed him with so many good things, and Dylan wanted to give something back to God.

Sharing and giving to others helps people feel closer to God. It helps them to see His blessings more clearly.

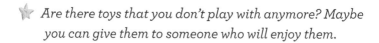 *Are there toys that you don't play with anymore? Maybe you can give them to someone who will enjoy them.*

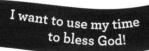 I want to use my time to bless God!

I Have Time

There is a right time for everything.

ECCLESIASTES 3:1

HERE IS A BLESSING THAT YOU MIGHT NOT HAVE THOUGHT ABOUT. Time! God blesses you and everyone else with time—seconds, minutes, hours, days, weeks, months, and years. God also blesses you with many ways to fill up your time. You can spend it playing, learning, sleeping, eating, helping, and doing many different things.

There is a right time for everything, and you should use your time wisely. When it is bedtime, then you should sleep. When it is time to get up, that is what you should do. You should spend your days playing and helping and learning.

In time, you will grow up to be a man or a woman, like your daddy or mommy. If you spend your time wisely, it will help you become the best grown-up you can be.

Spend time today learning something new. Then teach it to someone else.

Wherever I Am

Suppose I had wings . . . and flew across the ocean. Even then your powerful arm would guide and protect me.

PSALM 139:9–10 CEV

LONG AGO, THERE LIVED A MAN NAMED DAVID. He wrote songs about God. In one of his songs, David imagined what it would be like to have wings like a bird and fly. He said if he flew all the way across the ocean, God would be with him. God would go with him wherever he was and guide and protect him.

David knew that God blesses people by being with them wherever they go. Now you know it too. God is with you all the time wherever you go! In his song, David said that if he climbed all the way up into the sky or dug way down into the earth, God would be there.

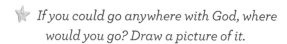 *If you could go anywhere with God, where would you go? Draw a picture of it.*

All the Time

"You can be sure that I will be with you always. I will continue with you until the end of the world."

MATTHEW 28:20

BEFORE JESUS WENT BACK TO HEAVEN, HE MADE A PROMISE. He promised people that He would always be with them.

You can't see Jesus or touch Him or hear Him. But Jesus can see you and hear you. He knows everything you do, and He loves you every minute of every day. He loves you so much that He can't take His eyes off you. Isn't that a wonderful blessing?

Jesus is with you all the time—not because He wants to spy on you, but because He wants you never to be alone. Jesus watches over you, and He promises to be with you all the days of your life.

Say this little prayer: "Thank You, Jesus, for watching over me all the time and for blessing me with Your love. Amen."

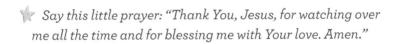

Thank You for being with me all the time, wherever I go.

Blessings Are Free

People are made right with God by his
grace, which is a free gift.

ROMANS 3:24

SOME PEOPLE BELIEVE THEY CAN EARN GOD'S BLESSINGS BY
ACTING IMPORTANT OR BEING VERY GOOD. But God blesses
people not because of who they are or how many good things they
do. He blesses them because He wants to and because He loves
them so much.

God's blessings are free. You don't have to earn them. God
blesses you with the air you breathe, sunshine, and fluffy, white
clouds in the sky. He blesses you with friends, family, and fun. God
is blessing you all the time with wonderful things. And every one of
them is free because He loves you!

*Use an old shoebox or other box to make a Family
Blessing Box. Each day, have family members write
down or draw a blessing to put in the box. After a month,
take the blessings out and count them together.*

God's blessings
are *free!*

God Has Time for Me

"God even knows how many hairs are on your head."
MATTHEW 10:30

THE WORLD IS A BUSY PLACE. People are busy. Sometimes moms and dads and brothers and sisters are so busy that they don't take time for each other.

There is One who is never too busy for you—God. He has the amazing, incredible power to be everywhere and do everything all at the same time. No matter how many other things God has to do, He always has time for you. If you don't believe it, think about this: God knows exactly how many hairs are on your head. Yes, He does! God has so much time to spend with you that He counts all your hairs. God blesses you with His time by knowing everything that goes on with you and helping you every minute of the day.

Time is a blessing, a special gift from God. Spend time with your family and friends today.

Today's Blessings

The Lord's love never ends. His mercies never stop. They are new every morning.

LAMENTATIONS 3:22-23

EACH NEW DAY IS A BLESSING. When you wake up in the morning, the day is like a blank piece of paper waiting for you to fill it up.

Lily has a play date today. Her friend Anna is coming over. The girls plan to make friendship bracelets. Trenton has a special day planned. He and his dad are going to the beach to fly kites. Trenton's dad made their kites, and Trenton is excited to see if they fly. Rita and her mom are helping today. They are going to their church to help at a bake sale.

God blesses you with many different ways to fill up your day. Don't forget to make Him a part of it. Spend time talking with God and thinking about His blessings.

 Try doing something today that you have never done before.

God Gives Me His Best

Since he did not spare even his own Son but gave him
up for us all, won't he also give us everything else?

ROMANS 8:32 NLT

OWEN LIKES TO EAT CERTAIN THINGS. He wants to have pizza,
soda, and cookies every day. But Owen's mom doesn't always give
him what he wants. Instead, she gives him what she knows is best
for him to grow up healthy and strong.

God gives His best to you too. When you ask God for what you
want, He might say no. God has your whole life planned out. The
parts of His plan for you connect like a puzzle. Sometimes you
might ask for something that doesn't fit into God's plan. If He says
no to you, don't feel bad. God does it because He loves you. He
loves you so much that He will always give you what's best.

*Say this little prayer: "Thank You, God, for
always giving Your best to me. Amen."*

I am grateful that God has planned
my entire life—today and every day!

69

Waiting for Blessings

You are wonderful, and while everyone watches, you store up blessings for all who honor and trust you.

PSALM 31:19 CEV

MACKENZIE IS LOOKING FORWARD TO HER BIRTHDAY. Her mom and dad told her that they have a special surprise for her. Mackenzie is excited just thinking about what it might be. She knows she will have a party with cake, ice cream, and presents. But there is something else. A secret. Mackenzie can't wait to find out what it is.

God has secrets too. He stores up blessings for people. Then, whenever He wants to, He gives His blessings away, like little gifts. You never know what God will bless you with or when. Waiting can be hard. But part of the fun is waiting and wondering what God's blessing might be. Waiting makes you think more about God and remember that each of His blessings is worth waiting for.

 What do you suppose is Mackenzie's birthday surprise?

Thank You, Lord, for giving so many special gifts.

Tomorrow's Blessings

"Don't worry about tomorrow. It will take care of itself. You have enough to worry about today."

MATTHEW 6:34 CEV

PEOPLE SOMETIMES WORRY ABOUT TOMORROW. They imagine all sorts of things that could happen. The truth is that most of the time, those things will not happen at all. God has everything under control. He knows exactly what tomorrow will be like.

God knows how the weather will be tomorrow. He knows where you will go and what you will do. He knows if you will be happy tomorrow or sad. God knows *right now* about every minute of tomorrow and the ways He will bless you.

Jesus said, "Don't worry about tomorrow." So enjoy today. Remember that God is working out His special plan for you, and it is a good plan. When you think about tomorrow, don't worry. Think of all the ways God might bless you.

⭐ *Draw a picture of something you look forward to doing tomorrow.*

71

Some Things Take Time

Faith means being sure of the things we hope for.
HEBREWS 11:1

OLIVER FELT DISAPPOINTED. He had looked forward to riding the big roller coaster at the amusement park. But when Oliver and his family got there, they discovered that Oliver could not ride. The man in charge said that Oliver was too short. Oliver wanted to grow two inches right then and there. But he couldn't! Some things take time.

God knows when is exactly the right time to bless someone with what he or she wants. As much as Oliver wanted to ride, it was not the right time. He might have been hurt if he did not obey the rules.

Oliver has faith in God. He is sure that one day when he is tall enough, God will bless him with a safe ride. In the meantime, Oliver will try to be patient and wait.

*What special thing do you want to do
when you are a little bit older?*

Be Patient

Wait and trust the Lord.

PSALM 37:7

BEING PATIENT IS ONE OF THE HARDEST THINGS FOR KIDS—AND GROWN-UPS TOO. Sometimes people want their blessings all at once! They want blessings to come down from heaven like rain. But God knows better. He knows that patience is a blessing.

The Bible says that waiting for something helps to make you strong—not strong like picking up your older brother and carrying him around all day, but strong in patience. God knows that learning to wait will make you a more patient person.

Patience is a good thing. A patient dad knows that it will take a while for you to learn to ride a two-wheeled bike. A patient teacher helps you for as long as it takes to understand something. A patient YOU knows that God's blessings are worth waiting for.

Make up a story about someone being patient.
Share it with your family and friends.

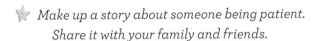

Learning to be patient
is a gift from God.

God Thinks About Me

God, your thoughts are precious to me. They are so many! If I could count them, they would be more than all the grains of sand.

PSALM 139:17–18

IMAGINE GOING TO A SANDY BEACH AND TRYING TO COUNT EACH LITTLE GRAIN OF SAND. That would be impossible! But God knows how many grains of sand there are. God knows that, and He knows all about you too. God thinks about you all the time.

Remember who God is. He is the great Creator who made heaven and earth. He is the King of kings and the one and only God. You must be very important to Him if He is always thinking about you.

God's thoughts about you are so many—more than all the grains of sand on all the beaches in the world! That's how much God loves you. His love is the greatest blessing of all.

 Draw a sand castle. Have you ever made a real one?

I'm so grateful God thinks about me and says I'm important.

I Am Worth It

*"Aren't two sparrows sold for only a penny? . . .
You are worth much more than many sparrows."*
MATTHEW 10:29–31 CEV

A SPARROW IS A SMALL, BROWN BIRD. You probably have seen sparrows near where you live. They like to visit people's yards and bird feeders.

Long ago, when Jesus lived on earth, people could buy sparrows two for a penny. Today, people don't buy sparrows. There are billions of sparrows in the world. Imagine if each one was worth a penny? To buy them all would cost a *lot* of money.

Jesus said that *you* are worth more to God than all those sparrows. God made you, and you are precious to Him. God would not trade you for all the money there ever was or ever will be. That is how much you mean to God. Isn't that a wonderful blessing?

 *The next time you go outside, look for sparrows or other kinds of birds. Count the ones you see.*

75

So Delighted

The LORD has done great things. All who take delight in
what he has done will spend time thinking about it.

PSALM 111:2 NIRV

AMY AND HER BEST FRIEND, GRACE, HAD A TEA PARTY.

"Would you care for a cup of tea?" asked Amy.

"I would be so delighted," Grace said in her best tea party voice.

Delighted is a word that means very happy. Amy would be very
happy to have a cup of tea with Grace.

When God blesses people, they feel delighted. Blessings make
people feel warm and good inside, like sharing a cup of tea with a
friend. God delights people by being with them wherever they go. And
everywhere they go, God blesses them in ways that make them joyful.

God will be delighted today if you think about His blessings.
Will you do that? Think about them all day long.

⭐ *Name three blessings that make you very joyful.*
Say a little prayer to thank God for them.

Pay Attention!

God watches where people go. He sees every step they take.
JOB 34:21

HAVE YOU EVER FELT LIKE AN ANT ON A SIDEWALK? There you are, working hard, when a big, black shadow falls across your path. You look up and see the bottom of someone's shoe. Oh no! You had better run fast. Don't you wish people would pay more attention?

Everyone forgets to pay attention sometimes—everyone except God. He never forgets to pay attention. Many times each day, God keeps you from trouble and you don't even know it. He is always watching out for you. That is another of His wonderful blessings. He sees you, hears you, and pays attention to you. God pays attention to you even when you are not paying attention to Him. He pays attention when you are awake and asleep and especially when you say your prayers.

⭐ *Name three ways you can pay attention to God.*

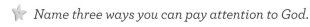

God blesses me by paying close attention to me.

Just as I Am

Yes, I am sure that nothing can separate
us from the love God has for us.

ROMANS 8:38

PLAYING DRESS-UP MAKES AMY AND GRACE FEEL HAPPY. When they dress up, they can be whatever they want. They pretend to be princesses, singers, doctors, teachers, and zookeepers. Sometimes they dress up Amy's little brother and let him play too. Dressing up is fun. It lets you imagine what it is like to be a grown-up.

The only One who knows what you will be when you grow up is God. He already has that planned for you. In time, you will know His plan. But whatever you end up doing, God will love you.

Do you know that God loves you just the way you are? You do not have to pretend to be something that you aren't to please Him. God loves you just because you're YOU!

 Name three things you like about yourself.

Thank You, God, for loving
me just the way I am!

Big, Squeezy Hugs

He tends his flock like a shepherd: He gathers the
lambs in his arms and carries them close to his
heart; he gently leads those that have young.

ISAIAH 40:11 NIV

WHEN ISAAC'S DADDY GETS HOME FROM WORK, HE OPENS HIS
ARMS UP WIDE AND SAYS TO ISAAC, "BIG, SQUEEZY HUG!" Isaac
knows what that means. He runs to his daddy. Then Daddy sweeps
Isaac off his feet. He holds Isaac tight, but not too tight, and gives
him a long, warm hug. Isaac's daddy gives the best hugs ever. His
hugs are a blessing. With those big, strong arms wrapped around
Isaac, holding him close, Isaac knows that his daddy loves him.

Do you know that God hugs you too? You can't feel God's arms
around you, like a daddy's hug, but whenever you feel loved and
protected, that's God hugging you and blessing you with His love.

*Give someone you love
a big, squeezy hug.*

79

Please, May I?

Pray and ask God for everything you need.
And when you pray, always give thanks.

PHILIPPIANS 4:6

GOD BLESSES YOU WITH A SPECIAL WAY TO TALK WITH HIM—PRAYER. You can pray to God about anything at all, and He promises to listen.

Last night, Makayla talked with God about school. Landon talked with Him about his T-ball game. Evan asked God to take care of his grandpa in the hospital.

God wants you to ask Him for whatever you need. When you ask, you can say, "Please, God, may I . . . ?" and then say whatever it is that is on your mind. Before you ask, think: Are you asking for something that you really need? God will decide how to answer. He will do what is good for you. That is because He loves you, and He knows best how to bless you.

When you pray today, ask God for what you need and thank Him for His blessings.

God Hears My Thoughts

The Lord knows what is in every person's mind.
He understands everything you think.

1 CHRONICLES 28:9

CALEB KNEELED DOWN TO PRAY. "Dear God! Help me to be good!" he shouted.

Caleb's mother looked at Caleb, surprised. "Caleb," she said, "why are you shouting?"

"Because I want God to hear me," said Caleb.

Caleb thought if he shouted his prayer, God would be sure to hear him.

You don't need a loud voice to pray to God. You don't need any voice at all! One of God's amazing blessings is that He hears everything you think. When you think a prayer in your head, it is called a silent prayer. God hears it just as if you were talking out loud.

You can talk with God all day long without saying one word. Give it a try. Wherever you are, God will hear you.

⭐ *God hears everything you think, so practice thinking about good things.*

It is a blessing to be able to talk to God.

I Am Loved

Three things continue forever: faith, hope and love. And the greatest of these is love.

1 CORINTHIANS 13:13

WHO LOVES YOU? Mommy and Daddy, brothers and sisters, grandparents, aunts, uncles, cousins, friends. Many people love you! That is because you are so lovable.

Love is the greatest gift of all. Do you know why? Because God is love! Everything about God is loving.

God blesses people with His patient love. He blesses them with love that is kind. God's love always forgives. He does not count up the wrong things people do and then take His love away. God is never selfish with His love. He gives it away to everyone, and He loves each person forever.

God wants you to love others the same way He does. And He wants others to love you with His kind of love.

⭐ *Draw a picture of yourself. Add these words: "I Am Loved."*

This Very Minute

The LORD will bless those who respect him,
from the smallest to the greatest.

PSALM 115:13 NCV

GABE WAS HELPING HIS MOTHER IN THEIR FLOWER GARDEN.
"Mommy," said Gabe. "How long does it take for a blessing to get
here from heaven?"

"No time at all," said his mother. "God blesses everyone who
loves Him. He sends them His blessings every minute of every day.
Look around you, Gabe. What blessings do you see?"

Gabe saw all kinds of blessings! His mommy was a blessing.
So was the fuzzy caterpillar resting on a leaf. The sunshine was
a blessing, and the flowers, and the birds in the trees, and the
squirrels scampering through the garden. God put all of those
things there for Gabe to enjoy at that very minute.

*Try this. Have someone time you for one minute. How
many blessings can you find before the time runs out?*

Help me to bless others by loving
them the way God loves me.

So Cozy

I have learned to be satisfied with the things I have and with everything that happens.

PHILIPPIANS 4:11

LUCIANA LOVED FRIDAY NIGHTS. Those were the nights she spent alone with her mommy. Friday nights were special because Luciana and her mommy got cozy together under a warm quilt and watched a movie. Sometimes they had popcorn. That made the night even more special. Luciana felt blessed to be so close to her mommy. It made her feel warm and good inside. She knew that she was safe and loved.

God's love makes you feel cozy and safe too. When you trust God, your heart fills up with His love. You feel good because you know that He is watching over you. When God fills up your heart with love, you know that you have everything you need and nothing can hurt you.

 Tell someone about a time when you felt cozy and safe.

All Together Now

It is good and pleasant when God's
people live together in peace!

PSALM 133:1

SATURDAY WAS A LAZY DAY AT MAX'S HOUSE. Rain poured down outside, and inside there was nothing to do. Max felt bored. So did his sister. Their mommy and daddy felt bored too.

Max had an idea. While his family sat around doing nothing, Max found games the whole family could play. Then he went into the kitchen and made some snacks.

"Hey, everybody!" said Max. "Come to the kitchen for a big surprise."

Max and his family played games and had fun just being together. Their boring rainy day turned into a happy one.

Family time on a rainy day is a blessing. Family time on *any* day is a blessing. Spending time together helps a family's love grow strong.

Does your family spend much time together?
Ask your parents to make time each week
for your family to do something fun.

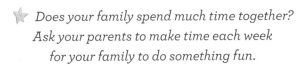

I'm so grateful God gives me
time with my family.

God Understands Me

Our LORD is great and powerful! He understands everything.
PSALM 147:5 CEV

JAYDEN'S DADDY HAD TWO TICKETS TO A BALL GAME. He planned to go with a friend. Jayden was not happy. He wanted to go too.

"Why can't I go?" Jayden asked.

"Because I am going with a friend," said his daddy.

"But why can't I go too?" said Jayden.

"I only have two tickets," his daddy answered. "You and I have been to games, and we will go again."

Jayden felt disappointed. "Nobody understands me!" he said. "I want to go!"

Jayden might feel like no one understands him, but God does. God understands everything. He blesses people by understanding what they want and what they need. He always makes the right decisions. Sometimes you might not like what God decides, but He knows best, and He loves you.

When you feel disappointed, you can trust God to understand. Talk with Him about it. He will help you feel better.

Thank You, God, for always understanding me.

Puppy Love

You are my hiding place. You protect me from my troubles.

PSALM 32:7

LAURA HAS A PUPPY NAMED SCAMP. The puppy is a lot like a human baby. It needs much love and care. In the daytime, Laura spends time with Scamp. She pets him and holds him. Scamp feels so safe in Laura's arms that sometimes he falls asleep. At nighttime when the family is sleeping, Scamp cries because he feels lonely and afraid. He looks for a safe place to hide. Scamp runs to Laura's bed and barks. Then Laura takes Scamp into bed and cuddles him.

Sometimes people wish they had a safe place to hide. When that happens, the best place to go is to God. He is the safest place of all. God blesses people by helping them feel loved and protected, like Scamp feels when he cuddles in Laura's arms.

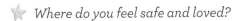 *Where do you feel safe and loved?*

Let's Play!

"And the streets will be filled with boys and girls playing."
ZECHARIAH 8:5

GOD LOVES KIDS! And He knows that kids love to play. God blesses kids with playgrounds that have swings and slides to play on. He blesses them with parks where they can run and play ball. God blesses kids with beaches where they can build sand castles. And with snow, so they can build snowmen. God blesses kids with zoos where they can see wild animals. And with pets to enjoy, and outside games, and with puzzles and board games for rainy days.

Best of all, God blesses kids with playmates. Play is more fun with friends. Playmates enjoy pretending and sharing their toys. They like sleepovers, doing crafts together, and exploring new places and things. And they especially like knowing that every day, God has more fun planned for them.

Name three new ways that you and your friends can have fun.

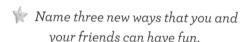

I'm thankful God loves to see me laugh and play.

88

So Silly!

Being wise is certainly better than being foolish.
ECCLESIASTES 2:13

"IAN, BREAKFAST IS READY," SAID HIS MOMMY.

Ian was in his room planning something silly. "I'll be right there!" Ian said. Then Ian put mittens on his bare feet and socks on his hands, and he went to the kitchen.

Ian's mommy didn't notice his silly clothes. She was busy putting pancakes on a plate. Ian could not help himself—he started to giggle. That got his mommy's attention, and she giggled too.

"Oh, Ian!" she said when she saw his feet wearing mittens and his hands wearing socks. "You are the silliest boy I know!"

It is fun to be silly sometimes. But it would not be funny if Ian had been silly in church or in the grocery store. God blesses people with wisdom to know when the time is right. Do you know when is the right time to be silly?

 Tell someone about the silliest thing you have ever done.

89

When I Am Sick

The people who trust the Lord will become strong
again. . . . They will run without needing rest.
ISAIAH 40:31

SAM FELT SICK. His tummy felt like it was spinning around, and
his head ached.

"Let's get you into bed," said his mommy.

While Sam rested, his mommy read to him. Sometimes she put
her cool hand on Sam's forehead to see if he had a fever. She prayed
for Sam and asked God to make him well.

The Bible tells us that people who trust God will become strong
again. They will run without needing rest. That is exactly what
happened with Sam. After a day or two, he felt just fine.

God knows when people are sick. He hears when people pray for
them. God blesses the sick with helpers, like Sam's mommy, to help
them feel better.

*Do you know someone
who is sick? Say a prayer
for him or her today.*

All By Myself

"Look at the new thing I am going to do."
ISAIAH 43:19

VALERY FELT SO EXCITED. She was going to school for the very first time! The week before, she had seen her classroom and met her teacher. Valery's sister told Valery all about school. "You will love it," her sister said. "School is fun."

As much as Valery wanted to go to school, she was a little worried. She did not like that she would be in school by herself. She wished her mommy could go with her.

"Mommies don't go to school with their kids," Valery's sister said. "You will be fine by yourself. God will be with you."

And Valery was fine. Her teacher met her at the door, and in no time at all, Valery made friends with her classmates.

No kid ever goes to school alone. God blesses them by being with them on the first day of school . . . and forever.

Play school with your friends.
Take turns being the teacher.

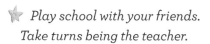

God blesses me by taking care of me—
especially when I'm sick or afraid.

Smiles

Happiness makes a person smile. But
sadness breaks a person's spirit.

PROVERBS 15:13

BRAYDEN SAT IN THE CAR ALL DRESSED UP AND FEELING SAD.
His family was on their way to have their picture taken for church.
Brayden did not want to go. He did not like having his picture taken.
He frowned all the way to church. He frowned when it was time for
the picture. He frowned when the photographer said, "Smile!"

"Come on, Brayden. Smile," said the photographer.

Then the photographer told jokes. They were the funniest jokes
Brayden had ever heard. Soon, he forgot about being sad. Brayden
smiled a big, happy smile, and the picture turned out fine.

God blesses people with many happy things to think about.
Whenever you feel sad, think about something happy. See if you
can turn your frown into a smile.

*Name three ways you can help turn
someone's frown into a smile.*

Laughter is a blessing!

That's Funny!

Be full of joy in the Lord always.
PHILIPPIANS 4:4

GOD MADE FUNNY THINGS TO BLESS PEOPLE WITH SMILES AND LAUGHTER.

Think about God's funny animals. Monkeys use their long arms to swing from trees and vines. They do somersaults and make silly faces. Elephants have trunks instead of noses. They fill up their trunks with water and shoot the water out. Penguins look like they are wearing suits. Ostriches are nine feet tall. They can't fly, but they run like the wind. Bats sleep hanging upside down. And have you seen a picture of a platypus? It is a furry animal that has a bill like a duck!

God made some funny plants too. There are plants that catch bugs and plants that are so stinky that you have to hold your nose.

Look all around you today. Maybe you will see something funny that God made just for you.

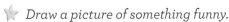

Draw a picture of something funny.

Friends Who Pray

Confess your sins to each other and pray for each other.
JAMES 5:16

ANOTHER OF GOD'S BLESSINGS IS PEOPLE WHO PRAY. If you are in trouble, other people can ask God to help you. If you are in danger, they can pray for your safety. If you are worried, they can ask God to help you feel calm. When you feel sick, people can ask God to make you well again.

Everyone needs people who pray. God wants families and friends to pray for each other. He blesses them with the gift of prayer. God wants to hear from people any time of the night or day. He is never too busy.

It is important to be honest and to tell others how they can pray for you. Don't be afraid to tell the truth. Is something bothering you today? Ask your family and friends to pray for you.

 Who can you pray for today?

The Lord blesses with friends who pray for us.

Pleasant Words

Pleasant words are like a honeycomb. They make a person happy and healthy.

PROVERBS 16:24

PAULINA'S MOMMY WAS BUSY DOING LAUNDRY. Clothes were everywhere—dirty clothes in baskets waiting to be washed, clothes in the washing machine, clothes in the dryer, and clothes waiting to be folded. All of that laundry made Paulina's mommy grumpy.

"Can I help you?" Paulina asked when she saw how busy her mommy was.

"Yes, please," said her mommy. "You are very kind, Paulina."

While they worked, Paulina and her mommy talked about pleasant things. When the laundry was done, they both felt good and ready to do something fun.

Pleasant talk means talking about good things. Pleasant talk is a blessing from God. Paulina and her mommy's pleasant conversation made the work go faster. Their talk was sweet like honey. It helped turn grumpiness into happiness.

⭐ Please *and* thank you *are pleasant words. Can you think of others?*

God's Best Medicine

A happy heart is like good medicine.
PROVERBS 17:22

DID YOU KNOW THAT GOD CREATED LAUGHTER? God made people to be joyful and happy. Laughing helps with that. When you feel sad and something makes you laugh, you feel better. Laughter is another of God's blessings.

Some people go around feeling sad all the time. But they don't have to. If they let God into their hearts, they can turn their sadness into joy. People can learn to think about God's blessings instead of their own troubles. They can chase their sadness away by looking for things that make them laugh.

You can find God's gift of laughter by being around happy people. When they laugh, you will start laughing too. The Bible says that a happy heart is like good medicine. It makes the sadness go away.

Name three things that make you laugh.
Think about them whenever you feel sad.

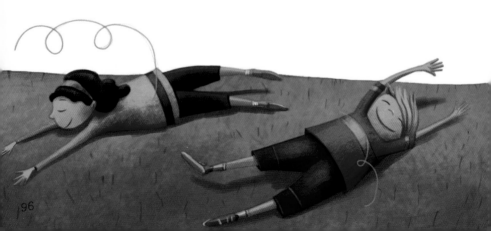

Friends Who Help

"I will make you strong and will help you."
ISAIAH 41:10

LONG AGO, A GREAT LEADER NAMED MOSES HELPED GOD'S PEOPLE TRAVEL TO A PLACE CALLED THE PROMISED LAND. On the way, they had a fight with an army that wanted to stop them. Moses and his friends Aaron and Hur climbed to a hilltop so they could see everything that went on. Then a strange thing happened. When Moses held up his arms, his army was winning the fight. But when he put his arms down, his army began to lose.

After a while, Moses' arms got so tired that he could not hold them up. Then Aaron and Hur helped. They held up Moses' arms for him. Isn't it wonderful that God blessed Moses with such helpful friends?

God blesses you with helpful friends too. And God is the best Helper of all. He promises to always help you and make you strong.

Who is your most helpful friend?

God, help me to bless others by being a helper.

Pleasing God

Everyone has sinned. No one measures up to God's glory.
ROMANS 3:23 NIRV

PARKER TRIED HIS BEST TO PLEASE GOD. But sometimes he messed up. Whenever Parker messed up, he felt bad. "I'll never be good enough for God," he said. "God must be mad at me!"

If Parker knew God better, he might not feel so bad. God wants people to obey and try their best at whatever they do. But God knows that sometimes people mess up. When people mess up and are sorry, God blesses them with His forgiveness. He never stops loving them.

Remember that God sent Jesus to take away people's sins. It is because of Jesus that people are forgiven when they disobey and get into trouble. Think about a time when you messed up. Did you remember then that God still loves you?

Say this little prayer: "Thank You, God, for loving me all the time, even when I disobey. Amen."

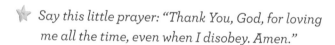
God forgives me when I make mistakes.

My Very Big Family

Yet some people accepted him and put their faith in him. So he gave them the right to be children of God.

JOHN 1:12 CEV

GOD BLESSES US WITH PARENTS. Your mommy's and daddy's parents are your grandparents. Your grandparents have parents and their parents had parents . . . and on and on, all the way back to the beginning! All of those people are your family. Some of them live here on earth, and others live in heaven now.

God invites people to be a part of His family too. You can become a part of God's family by believing that Jesus died for your sins. As a member of God's family, someday you will live with Him in heaven with other family members who are already there. All of you are God's children, and He will bless you by loving you forever.

Ask your parents and grandparents to tell you what they know about your family.

Honor Your Parents

Children, obey your parents the way the Lord
wants. This is the right thing to do.
EPHESIANS 6:1

YOUR MOMMY AND DADDY ARE GOD'S GIFT TO YOU, AND YOU
ARE GOD'S GIFT TO THEM. All of you are His blessings!

Mommies and daddies are God's special helpers. God puts them
in charge of taking care of their children and teaching them right
from wrong. Their job can be hard sometimes, especially when kids
disobey. God knows that. He made up a rule just for kids: *Honor
your father and mother.* You honor your mommy and daddy by
listening to them, forgiving them when they make mistakes, and
loving them. You also honor them by showing them respect and
obeying their rules.

When kids honor their parents, then everyone gets along and
home is a fun place to be.

⭐ *Make a picture or card to give
to your mommy and daddy. Tell
them that you love them.*

True Love

My children, our love should not be only words and talk. Our love must be true love. And we should show that love by what we do.

1 JOHN 3:18

WHEN FOSTER AND HIS MOMMY SAY, "I LOVE YOU," THEY REALLY MEAN IT. They know that true love is more than words. They show their love for each other by being kind, patient, unselfish, and forgiving.

One of God's special helpers was a man named Paul. He said, "If I did not love others, I would be nothing more than a clanging cymbal." Can you imagine the words "I love you" sounding like *CLANG, CLANG, CLANG,* or *CRASH, CRASH, CRASH?*

"I love you, Mommy," says Foster.

"I love you more," says his mommy.

When they say, "I love you," their words sound gentle and sweet. That is because they are blessed with God's love in their hearts, and they treat each other with love.

Show your family you love them today by doing kind and loving things.

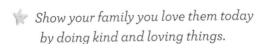

Mommies and daddies are wonderful gifts!

Let's Make Memories

He also said that you always have happy memories of us and that you want to see us as much as we want to see you.

1 THESSALONIANS 3:6 CEV

CASEY'S GRANDMA LIVES FAR AWAY. Whenever she comes to visit, Grandma says, "Let's make some memories!" Casey's grandma is good at making memories. She plans fun things for her and Casey to do together.

Casey and her grandma make scrapbooks with photos of things they do. They walk in the woods, and Grandma teaches Casey the names of wildflowers and of birds they see in the trees. They bake together too. Grandma shares her favorite cookie recipes with Casey.

When it is time for Grandma to go, she says, "Casey, hold those memories tight until I see you again."

Memories are a special blessing from God. They help people feel like they are together even when they live apart.

 Draw a picture of something good that you remember.

Thank You, God, for giving me a mind that can make memories.

God's Love Letter

All Scripture is given by God.
2 TIMOTHY 3:16

GOD WROTE HIS CHILDREN A LOVE LETTER. It is called the Bible, and it is filled with His blessings.

God's helpers wrote down God's words for everyone to read. The Bible tells about how much God loves people. It tells about the wonderful things He does to show them His love. The Bible also teaches people how to live because God always knows what is best for them.

One part of the Bible is all about Jesus. It has true stories about when Jesus was born, what He did to teach and help people, and how He died so God's people could live in heaven someday.

The Bible is the most important book of all. Do you have a Bible in your house?

Have someone help you write a love letter to God.
Ask that person to read it out loud for God to hear.

God Cares for Me

"You, my human sheep, are the sheep I care for, and I am your God."

Ezekiel 34:31 NCV

PETS ARE LOVED LIKE MEMBERS OF A FAMILY. Good pet owners take care of their pets. They give them food, water, and whatever else they need.

The Bible tells a story about a poor man who lived long ago. He and his children owned a pet lamb. They didn't have much money, but they took care of their lamb. They shared their food and water with it. The little lamb slept in the man's arms, and the Bible says that the lamb was like a daughter to him. The man loved his little lamb, and he gave it good care.

Do you know that God is the best caregiver of all? He says His people are like little lambs that He loves. He blesses and cares for them because He is their God.

Do you have a pet? Are you a good caregiver?

⭐ *Name three things that all pets need.*

Cars, Buses, Trains, and Planes

We all knelt down on the beach and prayed.
Then we said good-bye and got on the ship.
ACTS 21:5-6

TRAVELING WAS NOT EASY WHEN JESUS LIVED ON EARTH. There were no cars, buses, trains, or airplanes. Most of the time, people walked. Sometimes they walked for many days and for many miles. Sometimes they rode on mules or on big humpbacked camels. When people needed to go across the sea, they sailed on wooden ships. The ships had a hard time sailing in strong winds and rough waters. People prayed, asking God to keep them safe.

Today, God blesses people with easy ways to travel. Airplanes and big, strong ships take people safely over water. Cars, buses, and trains help them travel across land. Traveling many miles can take just hours instead of days.

When you pray today, tell God, "Thank You for cars, buses, trains, and planes."

 Draw a picture of your favorite way to travel.

God shows His love by going with me and caring for me.

A First Time for Everything

Young people, enjoy yourselves while you are
young. Be happy while you are young.

ECCLESIASTES 11:9

GOD KNOWS THAT KIDS LIKE TO ENJOY THEMSELVES AND BE
HAPPY. That is one reason that He blesses them with first times. If
kids don't try new things, they won't know whether they like them.
First times can be exciting. They help kids discover many new
things to enjoy.

Do you remember the first time you had a party? How about the
first time you went swimming or the first time your family went on
a vacation?

God has plenty of fun things waiting for you, so don't be afraid
to try. Maybe you will go to new places and meet new playmates.
Maybe you will ride on an airplane, an elephant, or maybe a giant
roller coaster. Surely you will see things you haven't seen before.
There is a first time for everything!

What new thing have you tried lately?

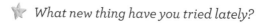

I'm grateful God lets me
experience exciting new things!

106

An Exciting Surprise

I will sing joyful praises and be filled with excitement.
PSALM 63:5 CEV

MATEO'S MOMMY AND DADDY HAD A SURPRISE FOR HIM. "We are taking a vacation!" Mateo's mommy said. "Next week, we are going to see the ocean."

Mateo was very excited. He had never been to the ocean. "What will it be like?" Mateo asked. "Can we go swimming? Will we see a shark or a dolphin?"

Mateo's mommy said, "You will have to wait and see."

Mateo knew that God was blessing him with an adventure, and he looked forward to whatever God had planned for him. That night, when Mateo kneeled down to pray, he thanked God for blessing him with such a wonderful surprise. He even sang a song to God because he was so happy.

Do you remember to thank God when He surprises you with something grand?

Tell someone about a time when God blessed you with a surprise.

God Made the Ocean

The earth was barren, with no form of life; it was under a roaring ocean covered with darkness. But the Spirit of God was moving over the water.

GENESIS 1:2 CEV

"DADDY," SAID MATEO. "Who made the ocean?"

"God did," his daddy said. "Before the earth had people, it was under a roaring ocean. God had made the ocean. He was watching over it, and everything was dark. Then God turned the darkness into daytime. He made the sky, and He moved all the water into one place. He made the ground and named it *land,* and He named the water *ocean.* God looked at what He had done, and He said, 'This is good!'"

Mateo thinks the ocean is an awesome blessing. It is so big that you cannot see across it no matter how hard you try. It is very deep and filled with wonderful things waiting to be discovered.

What do you think Mateo will discover when he goes to the ocean?

God blessed us with His amazing creation, including the ocean and the beach!

At the Beach

"I am the one who made the beaches
to be a border for the sea."

JEREMIAH 5:22

MATEO COULD NOT BELIEVE HIS EYES WHEN HE SAW THE OCEAN. It was more wonderful than he had imagined. He explored its sandy beach. He discovered all kinds of things that God had made. He found beautiful seashells, a starfish, and colorful sea glass. He saw crabs skittering across the sand and snails moving slowly near the water. He found animal and bird tracks along the water's edge. Mateo's daddy showed him some strange tracks made by a sea turtle. There was old wood on the beach covered with seaweed. Mateo wondered if it came from an ancient sailing ship.

Mateo met new playmates on the beach too. They showed him holes made by ghost crabs and places where sea turtles had buried their eggs.

His whole day was filled with God's blessings!

⭐ *Draw a picture of yourself at the beach.*

Underwater

Then God said, "Let the water be filled with living things."
GENESIS 1:20

MATEO AND HIS FAMILY WENT TO A MUSEUM NEAR THE
OCEAN. There they learned about some of the wonderful blessings
that God hid underwater. Scientists say there are millions of
animals and plants that live in the ocean. God made them all.

Mateo learned about whales, sharks, and dolphins. He saw
pictures of colorful fish and coral that grow on the ocean floor. He
found out that jellyfish sting and squid shoot out a black liquid that
looks like ink. Octopuses live in the ocean, and so do shrimp. There
are very tiny animals living in the water. At night, they come to the
water's edge. Their bodies glow in the dark! Mateo could not wait
until nighttime so he could see them.

"Thank You, God, for the ocean!" Mateo said. "And thank You for
everything that lives in it."

 Which is your favorite ocean animal?

God, I thank You for eyes
that can see and a mind that can learn.

What Do You See?

He has made everything beautiful in its time.
ECCLESIASTES 3:11 NIV

CONNOR'S TEACHER SAID, "WHAT IS THE MOST BEAUTIFUL THING YOU HAVE EVER SEEN?" Connor answered, "The big parrot that lives in the zoo." Elizabeth said, "My grandma's pretty flower garden." Akin said the most beautiful thing he has ever seen is the lake where he and his grandpa go fishing.

God blesses people with eyes so they can see all the lovely things He puts in the world. There is so much to look at: seashells on the beach, stars in the sky, mountains, valleys, woodlands, and fields. There are tulips and buttercups, brightly colored bugs and butterflies, brown-spotted puppies, green-skinned frogs—so much to see!

What is the most beautiful thing you have ever seen?

⭐ *Look around you. Count the beautiful things you see. Say, "Thank You, God, for giving me eyes."*

Little Things

The Lord is great. He is worthy of our praise.
PSALM 145:3

SOME OF GOD'S BLESSINGS ARE SMALL. If you don't look closely, you might miss them.

Look closely at rocks along a beach or a stream, and you might find some fossils. Fossils are little marks left in rocks by animals that lived long ago. Take a look at tree branches in the spring before the leaves come out. You might see buds—tiny leaves waiting to grow. Pretty little bugs, like ladybugs, hang out on flowers. Have you seen them? If you go outside on a summer night, you might see fireflies blinking their lights. In winter, when it snows, catch a tiny snowflake on your mitten. Look closely. Do you see its pretty design? God made and scattered around many small things for you to discover.

Thank You, God, for little things!

 *Name three little things that God made.*

Big Things

*You, LORD God, have done many wonderful things,
and you have planned marvelous things for us.*

PSALM 40:5 CEV

SOME OF GOD'S BLESSINGS ARE BIG, LIKE THE OCEAN. People look at them and say, "Only God could make something as big and wonderful as that!" God made other big things too, like mountains and like trees that grow as tall as skyscrapers. Their trunks are so big that it would take you and nine friends holding hands to reach all the way around one! God made big animals too, like elephants and blue whales. Blue whales are the largest animals known to live on earth. The biggest ones are as long as two school buses and weigh as much as a bus filled with kids!

No human can ever make huge mountains, giant trees, or big blue whales. That is why God is so great. He can do anything!

⭐ *Tell someone about the biggest
thing you have ever seen.*

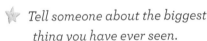

Little things and big things . . .
God made them all!

113

Wild Animals

**God made the wild animals, the tame animals,
and all the small crawling animals.**

GENESIS 1:25

HANNAH AND HER FAMILY HAD AN ADVENTURE. They went to a wild animal park where they could drive through and see the animals up close.

A tall van drove Hannah's family slowly through the park. Sometimes along the way it stopped. Fat black bears walked around the van and looked inside. So did zebras, elephants, wolves, and tigers. A striped red snake slithered through some leaves at the side of the road. Colorful birds, little and big, flew from tree to tree. Then a giraffe and her baby walked right up to the van, and the baby pressed its nose against Hannah's window.

"Look at the baby!" Hannah cried. "Look at all the animals!"

"Aren't they a blessing?" said Hannah's mommy. "And God made them all."

⭐ *Make the sound of your favorite animal.
See if someone can guess what it is.*

114

A Giant Roar

Be strong and brave. Don't be frightened.
DEUTERONOMY 31:6

HANNAH'S FAMILY'S TRIP TO THE WILD ANIMAL PARK WAS ALMOST OVER. The van took them through a winding road that went through a field of tall, golden grass.

"Oh, oh!" said the van's driver. "Here comes the king of the beasts."

A huge lion with a shaggy mane came out of the grass. It stood in the road in front of the van, and it did not look happy. Then the lion shook its head, and it let out a great big *ROAAAAAAAR!*

The big noise scared Hannah. She leaned against her mommy, and Mommy held Hannah close. "Be brave, honey," she said. "That lion isn't the king. God is."

Hannah's mommy was right. God is the King of Everything, even scary lions. God blesses people with bravery when they remember that He is King.

 Who helps you be brave when you feel afraid?

I'm thankful You made snakes that slither and lions that roar.

All God's Children

You are all the same in Christ Jesus.
GALATIANS 3:28

SOLOMON'S FAMILY WENT TO A FESTIVAL ABOUT PEOPLE FROM DIFFERENT COUNTRIES AROUND THE WORLD. The people dressed in costumes from their countries. They danced and sang songs. Solomon saw and heard things he had never seen or heard before.

"Daddy," he said, "why are these people so different? They don't look like us. They don't dance or talk like us either."

"They are all people, just like you and me," said Solomon's daddy. "People do things differently in different parts of the world. When God sees people, Solomon, He doesn't see them looking different. God sees them all alike. And if they believe in Jesus, then they are God's children. He blesses them with His love wherever they live in the world."

Solomon likes it that people do different things. It makes God's world an interesting place.

 Ask your parents to find some music from another country. Listen to it together.

I'm so grateful we are all God's children—in my town, my country, and the whole world!

God's Love Keeps Me Safe

*He will protect you like a bird spreading
its wings over its young.*

PSALM 91:4

DO YOU KNOW HOW A MOTHER BIRD PROTECTS HER BABIES?
She spreads her wings out wide. Then her babies hurry underneath
them. Under their mother's wings, the baby birds feel safe and loved.

The Bible tells us many wonderful things about God's love. It
says His love is like a mother bird covering her babies with her
wings. When danger is near, God uses His love to bless and protect
His children. His love helps them be brave and hopeful. It helps
them feel comfortable and safe.

Everyone feels afraid sometimes. When you feel afraid, you can
trust in God's love. Talk to Him, and He will help you feel calm.
Imagine Him wrapping His love all around you and holding you
close to His heart.

*Say this little prayer: "Dear God, thank You
for covering me up with Your love. Amen."*

"¡Hola! Hello!"

So the Lord scattered them from there over all the earth.
GENESIS 11:8

HAVE YOU WONDERED WHY PEOPLE LIVE IN DIFFERENT PLACES AND SPEAK DIFFERENT LANGUAGES? Long ago, everyone lived close together and spoke the same language. These people were full of themselves. They thought they could do great things just like God can. They began building a tower. They planned for it to reach way up into the sky. "We will be as great as God!" they said.

But no one can be as great as God. God saw, and He mixed things up. He gave the people different languages so they couldn't understand each other. Then they had to stop building. Soon, they moved to different places all over the world.

Whatever language you speak, God blesses you with His understanding. He understands everything you say, and He loves you.

*"¡Hola!" (oh-la) means "hello" in Spanish.
Teach this new word to a friend.*

118

Give It a Try

Christ accepted you, so you should accept
each other. This will bring glory to God.

ROMANS 15:7

AT THE FESTIVAL, SOLOMON DISCOVERED FOODS FROM
AROUND THE WORLD. He had tried some of them before, and
he knew he would like them. But then his mommy offered him
something called tong mandu. Solomon did not know what that
was, and he was afraid to try.

"Give it a little taste," said his mommy.

"No," said Solomon. "It has a funny name."

"Don't think about its name," she said. "Think of the good things
that might be in it."

So Solomon tried a little tong mandu, and he liked it!

God doesn't care about names. But He does care about what
is inside. That is especially true about people. When you meet
someone new, give him a try. See if he is good inside. You might
find that God has blessed you with a new friend.

 Tell someone about a time when you made a new friend.

God blesses us with mouths
that can taste new things!

God Gives Me Rest

"Come to me, all of you who are
tired. . . . I will give you rest."

MATTHEW 11:28

MATEO, HANNAH, AND SOLOMON HAD WONDERFUL ADVENTURES
AT THE BEACH, THE WILD ANIMAL PARK, AND THE FESTIVAL. But
after a while, they all were very tired. They wanted to go home.

God blesses people with homes where they feel safe and loved.
Home is a place where people can be comfortable and get some rest.

Rest is important to God. After He made the sky and the earth
and everything on it, God rested. Jesus made time to rest too. After
a busy day talking with people and helping them, Jesus often went
off by Himself to be quiet and rest.

Rest is a blessing. A little rest can chase away grumpiness. Best
of all, rest gives you energy so you can have more adventures.

*Find a little space that is all your own,
someplace where you can go to be quiet and rest.*

Let's Plant a Garden

There is a time to plant and a time to pull up plants.

ECCLESIASTES 3:2

WHEN GOD'S SPRING SUNSHINE WARMED UP THE EARTH, CLAIRE AND HER MOMMY MADE A GARDEN.

"First, we have to clean things up," said Claire's mommy. They raked up dead leaves and sticks and threw them away. Then they raked the soil nice and smooth. Claire and her mommy planted seeds. They planted vegetable seeds in one spot and flower seeds in another.

"Now we have to be God's helpers," said Mommy. "We have to take care of the garden and help the seeds grow."

God could take care of the garden all by Himself, but He wants people to be His helpers. God blesses people with seeds, and they plant the seeds and give them water and food to grow. When people help with the work, they grow closer to God.

 What kinds of seeds would you like to plant?

Thank You, God, for giving us plants that grow into food.

Hello, Sunshine!

Sunshine is sweet; it is good to see the light of day.
ECCLESIASTES 11:7 NCV

AFTER GOD MADE THE EARTH, HE PUT THE SUN IN THE SKY TO DIVIDE NIGHTTIME FROM DAYTIME. God made the sun very hot. He made the earth tilt toward the sun in the springtime. In springtime, the sunshine feels warmer. The sun warms things up and helps plants grow.

The sun is a big blessing. It gives the earth light and heat. Without the sun, life on earth could not exist. It would be so cold that nothing could stay alive. Earth would be one big, frozen ball.

The sun is so bright that looking at it directly is dangerous. But God thought of that too. He made sunrises and sunsets that people can look at. In the morning and evening, the sun turns the sky into beautiful, fiery colors.

Thank You, God, for sunshine!

 Name three good things about the sun.

Sunshine and spring remind me of God's gift of new life!

Wake Up! It's Spring

"Look! I am making everything new!"
REVELATION 21:5

WAKE UP! It's springtime. If you don't get up and look around, you might miss all of the little blessings God has hidden for you outside.

Look in the garden. You might see tulips and daffodils peeking their little, green tops through the soil. It's time for them to wake up after resting underground all winter long. Look closely and you might see a squirrel scurrying through the grass. It just woke up too, after a long sleep in its cozy winter home. In the woods, Mother Bear and her cub just woke up after sleeping through the winter. They are exploring and looking for food. Have you noticed the days getting longer? God planned it that way to bless farmers with more daylight to plant their fields.

What other spring blessings might there be?

Say this little prayer: "Thank You, God, for springtime blessings. Thank You, God, for waking things up! Amen."

Springtime Is for Easter

"Say to them: 'Jesus has risen from death.'"
MATTHEW 28:7

SPRINGTIME BRINGS THE BLESSING OF EASTER.

Easter is all about Jesus. It was a Friday when Jesus died on the cross. His friends put His dead body in a cave called a tomb. They blocked its door with a huge rock before they went away. Soldiers guarded Jesus' tomb day and night making sure that no one took His body away. But God did a miracle. On Sunday morning, God made Jesus' body come alive again! An angel rolled the stone away, and Jesus' body was gone. His friends saw Him walking around. "Look!" they said. "Jesus is alive!"

We remember that special day as Easter.

After a while, Jesus went up to heaven to be with His Father, God. But Jesus is still alive today. He is with us, just like God is. And do you know what else? Jesus loves you!

Ask someone to read you the Easter story from the Bible, in Matthew 28:1–20.

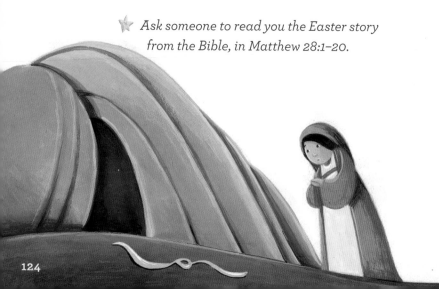

An Unexpected Problem

We know that in everything God works for the good of those who love him.

ROMANS 8:28

GOD SOMETIMES BLESSES PEOPLE WITH WONDERFUL LITTLE SURPRISES. That is what happened to Alex when he went outside after it rained. He had left his trucks in the dirt where he was digging a hole. God's rain shower filled up the hole and made it into a puddle. Oh, what fun Alex could have now! He pretended the puddle was a lake. He made sticks float on it, and he pretended they were boats. Alex's trucks carried things to and from the lake. The rain shower that had made Alex feel unhappy had been a surprise blessing from God. It made his playtime even more fun.

God sometimes hides little blessings in not-so-good days. When you have an unhappy day, look for God's blessings. He blesses you because He loves you!

 Make up a story about a time when God turned a bad day into a good one.

Sometimes God's blessings come in disguise.

Animal Babies Everywhere

Train a child how to live the right way. Then even
when he is old, he will still live that way.

PROVERBS 22:6

MANY BABY ANIMALS ARE BORN IN THE SPRING.

Listen and you might hear baby birds chirping inside their nests.
Watch and you might see their parents bringing them food. Their
parents teach them that good food is important. When the babies get
bigger, their parents will teach them to fly and find food on their own.

Listen and you might hear baby squirrels in the trees. *Chat-chat-chat!* they scold one another. Watch and you might see them
playing roly-poly on the ground. Their mother is watching. She
teaches them to find food, how to act around other animals, and
how to live on their own.

God blesses all animals and children with parents. It is the
parents' job to teach babies to grow up right and to care for
themselves.

 *Name three things that you have
learned from your parents.*

Thank You, Lord,
for baby animals.

God's Four Seasons

*To everything there is a season, a time
for every purpose under heaven.*
ECCLESIASTES 3:1 NKJV

GOD MADE FOUR SEASONS—SPRING, SUMMER, FALL, AND WINTER. He made each one different and filled it with wonderful blessings for people to enjoy.

God's first season, spring, is the time when plants and some animals wake up after sleeping through the winter months. In spring, the air becomes warmer and flowers begin to bloom. Summer comes next. It is the time when most kids are out of school and enjoying hot, sunny days. Then comes fall, when the air becomes cool. Fall is pumpkin time and time for the leaves on trees to change color. And last comes winter, with its cold days and snowmen and Christmas.

God made each season for a purpose, and each one is beautiful. Seasons change, but God does not. He blesses people by staying the same all the time.

 Which is your favorite season? Draw a picture of it.

Spring Showers

God takes up the drops of water from the earth.
And he turns them into drops of rain. Then
the rain pours down from the clouds.

JOB 36:27-28

ALEX HAD BEEN ENJOYING THE SPRING SUNSHINE. He was
playing in the dirt with his trucks until some ugly gray clouds
floated through the sky. The clouds covered up the sun, and
rain began to fall. Alex had to go inside. The rain made him feel
disappointed. He wanted to be outside playing with his trucks.

"It's only a spring shower," his mommy said. "It will be done in
no time. Rain is God's blessing. It helps the flowers grow."

The rain fell hard. *Pat-a-pat, pat-a-pat!* But it did not last long. The
clouds went away, and the sun shone brightly in the sky. That made
Alex happy. He could go outside again and play with his trucks.

*Riddle: What goes up when the rain
comes down? Answer: an umbrella!*

A Spring Suprise

Do not be interested only in your own life,
but be interested in the lives of others.

PHILIPPIANS 2:4

ONE SPRING DAY, MARTIN FOUND A BABY BIRD ON THE GROUND. It was so young that its feathers were like short whiskers. Martin knew better than to touch it. He ran to get his daddy.

"Let's find the nest," said Daddy. They looked up at the branches in a nearby tree. "I see it!" Daddy said. He pointed, and Martin saw it too. "Watch the bird while I get my ladder."

Martin watched the baby to make sure it stayed safe. When Daddy came back, he picked up the bird very gently. He climbed up the ladder and put the baby back in its nest. "It's a blessing that we were here to help," Daddy said.

God knows when unexpected problems happen, and He knows how to solve them. He blesses people with helpers.

 When you have a problem, whom can you go to for help?

God can use me to bless
and care for His creation.

An Unexpected Blessing

The Lord is great; he should be praised.

PSALM 96:4

SPRING WAS ALMOST OVER WHEN VICTORIA DISCOVERED A LITTLE BROWN SACK HANGING FROM A TREE BRANCH. *I wonder what it is,* she thought. Just then, Victoria's brother arrived home from school. "Ben, come see," said Victoria. "What is this funny little sack?"

"That is a pupa," said Ben. "First a butterfly laid some eggs. Caterpillars hatched from the eggs. Then a caterpillar made this little brown sack. It is inside, and something great is happening. One day soon, the pupa will split open and a butterfly will come out."

That's neat, Victoria thought. "Did the caterpillar make the butterfly?" she asked.

"No," Ben answered. "God turned the caterpillar into a butterfly. It's an unexpected blessing!"

God is so great. He can change caterpillars into butterflies, good into bad, and darkness into light. Can you think of other things that God can do?

Say this little prayer: "I praise You, God, because You are great. Amen."

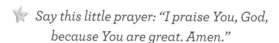

I can find blessings in hidden and unusual places!

Summertime

You made all the limits on the earth.
You created summer and winter.

PSALM 74:17

GOD'S NEXT SEASON IS SUMMER. The air and the earth are warmer in summer than in springtime. Seeds have grown into flowers and vegetables. Kids are out of school, playing, riding their bikes, and having adventures. People go to the beach or run through water sprinklers to stay cool. Cold lemonade helps too. Everywhere you look, things are changing so fast that it is hard to keep up. Baby birds have left their nests, and more babies have taken their places. Baby squirrels are all grown up and finding food on their own. Bright colors are everywhere on flowers, fruits, and vegetables. People go to picnics, light fireworks, and wave flags. There are parades to attend and festivals and fairs.

God made summertime so much fun, and He filled it with blessings for everyone!

Draw a picture of your favorite thing to do in the summer.

131

"No, No, No"

"You will hear a voice . . . say, 'This is the right way. You should go this way.'"

ISAIAH 30:21

ONE DAY, VICTORIA SAW A BEAUTIFUL BUTTERFLY RESTING ON A FLOWER. "I wonder if this is my butterfly from the pupa," Victoria said. She hurried to check the pupa she had found hanging from a tree branch. It was empty! "You *are* my butterfly!" Victoria cried. "I will keep you forever. I will make a little house for you to live in." So Victoria put the butterfly in a jar. "There," she said. "Now you have a safe place to live."

Just then, Victoria heard a little voice inside her heart. It said, "No, no, no." What do you think it meant?

God blesses people by reminding them about right and wrong. He was speaking to Victoria that day. When Victoria heard Him say, "No, no, no," it made her stop and think about right and wrong.

 What do you think God was trying to tell Victoria?

Fluttering butterflies are a beautiful blessing.

Fly Away

But the Lord said to me, "My grace is enough for you. When you are weak, then my power is made perfect in you."

2 CORINTHIANS 12:9

WHEN VICTORIA TRAPPED THE BUTTERFLY IN A JAR, A GENTLE VOICE WHISPERED IN HER HEART, "NO, NO, NO." Some people call that voice their "conscience." But Victoria knew it was God telling her that she had made a wrong choice.

Victoria had wanted to keep the butterfly safe. But butterflies are meant to be free. God made them to fly, not to live in jars. As much as Victoria wanted to keep the butterfly, she let it go. Victoria listened to God's voice. She gave the butterfly back to Him so He could take care of it. She remembered that God is very powerful, and His power is enough to care for the little butterfly.

God blesses everyone by caring for them in His own way.

Would you have kept the butterfly? Why or why not?

God's Power Supply

Even young people get tired. . . . But those who trust the LORD will find new strength.

ISAIAH 40:30–31 CEV

SUMMER IS A SEASON WHEN KIDS NEED LOTS OF ENERGY. There are bikes and scooters to ride, ball games to play, places to run to, and things to climb. The energy it takes to do all those things would make a grown-up tired. But kids, like you, just keep going.

Maybe your mommy or daddy has said to you, "Where do you get all that energy?" The answer is from God. He knows that kids want to play, so He blesses them with plenty of get-up-and-go. Energy is God's power supply. God knows exactly how much energy each person needs and when they need it. God gives kids an extra boost of energy so they can play all day long!

 Can you name three ways to use up some energy?

I'm grateful for all the energy God has given me.

Look Closely

But even there you can look for the Lord your God. And you will find him if you look. But you must look for him with your whole being.

DEUTERONOMY 4:29

THE BUTTERFLY WAS NOT THE ONLY VISITOR IN VICTORIA'S GARDEN. Had she looked closely, Victoria would have discovered many of God's little creatures living there. God puts good bugs in the garden to help keep the plants healthy and strong. Good bugs, like the butterfly, help spread pollen from plant to plant. Pollen helps fruits and vegetables grow. Bees help with pollen too. Other bugs, like ladybugs, spiders, and ground beetles, eat bad bugs to stop them from killing good plants. These bugs are God's blessings. He uses them to help care for the garden.

You will find God's blessings in the garden and all around you. But you must look closely. Some of them are hard to find.

Look at dirt and plants using a magnifying glass. What do you see?

135

Treasure Hunt

"I love those who love me. Those who want me find me."
PROVERBS 8:17

EZRA'S SUNDAY SCHOOL TEACHER PLANNED A FUN ACTIVITY FOR HIS CLASS. "This week, I'm sending you on a treasure hunt," the teacher said. "I want each of you to look all around you for God's blessings. Let's see how many blessings you can find."

Ezra worried that it might be hard to find blessings. But when he began looking, he found them easily. His house was a blessing. So were his parents and his brother and sister. His friends were blessings, and his pets were too. Ezra searched inside and out, and soon he had a long list of blessings.

God loves it when people look for and find Him. He says that anyone who searches for Him will find Him. People find God in all of His blessings. They find Him at home, at church, and wherever they go.

⭐ *Now it's your turn. Hunt for God's blessings. How many can you find?*

Winning Isn't Everything

Help me want to obey your rules instead
of selfishly wanting riches.

PSALM 119:36

MILES WAS RUNNING IN THE COUSINS' RACE AND WINNING
WHEN HE HEARD SOMEONE WAILING NEAR THE PLAYGROUND.
He saw one of his younger cousins on the ground and grown-ups
running toward her. Miles felt worried. Something was wrong. *I am
halfway to the finish line*, Miles thought, *and I know I can win this
race.* Then Miles heard his aunt yell, "Call 9-1-1!"

Miles had to make a quick decision. Should he keep running to
win, or should he help? *Winning isn't everything*, Miles thought.
My cousin is more important. So Miles kept running, but instead of
running for the finish line, he ran to the playground.

God had blessed Miles with the gift of love. His love for his
cousin was greater than his need to win the race.

 *What would you have done, finish
the race or help your cousin?*

We are blessed
when God sends help.

God Sends Help

Lord, be kind to me because I am weak. Heal me, Lord, because my bones ache.

PSALM 6:2

ONE OF MILES'S YOUNGER COUSINS FELL OFF A SWING AT THE FAMILY PICNIC. His mom, dad, aunts, and uncles rushed to help.

"My leg hurts!" the cousin cried.

"Call 9-1-1," an aunt shouted.

Everyone helped in their own way. Some helped by keeping the cousin calm. Others prayed for his leg to be well. An ambulance came with its lights flashing and siren wailing. It brought more helpers to take Miles's cousin to the hospital. Doctors and nurses at the hospital made the little boy feel much better. They put a cast on his broken leg and said that, before long, his leg would be fine. The whole family felt better when they heard the good news.

When accidents happen, God blesses people with His kindness. He sends others to help them.

Tell someone about a time when you got hurt and God sent help.

Run to Win

You know that in a race all the runners run. But only
one gets the prize. So run like that. Run to win!

1 CORINTHIANS 9:24

EVERY SUMMER, MILES'S WHOLE FAMILY—MOM, DAD, BROTHERS,
SISTERS, AUNTS, UNCLES, AND COUSINS—GET TOGETHER FOR A
PICNIC. They eat good food and play games. The best game is the
cousins' race, where all the cousins race for a prize. Miles was not a
very good runner, but he believed that he could get better and win
the next race. Miles trusted God to help him. Every day, all year long,
Miles practiced running. By picnic time he was ready.

The cousins stood on the starting line. One of the uncles
shouted, "Ready, set, go!" Miles ran hard. He ran to win. He did his
very best, and he ran faster than all of his cousins. God blessed
Miles because he had worked hard and done his best.

*Ask God to help you with something
you want to be better at.*

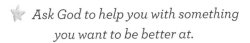

Blessings are all around us.

A Summer Plan

So God created human beings in his image.

GENESIS 1:27

"THERE IS NOTHING TO DO TODAY," JAZMIN SAID.

"I know," answered her best friend, Danna. "I am tired of games, riding my bike, and playing with toys. What else can we do?"

The girls thought for a while.

"I have an idea!" Jazmin said. "Let's put on a show. We can ask our friends to be in it. We can sing songs, do skits, and dance. Let's invite our parents and brothers and sisters to be the audience. It will be so much fun!"

The girls gathered their friends to help. Together, they imagined what their show would be like.

When God created people, He made them to be a lot like Him, to think and to have ideas. God has an endless supply of good ideas. He blesses people with imaginations so they can have good ideas too.

 Use your imagination today to make something or to put on a show for your family.

A good imagination is a great blessing!

Luck or Blessings?

People throw lots to make a decision. But
the answer comes from the Lord.

PROVERBS 16:33

EZRA FOUND SOME BLESSINGS OUTSIDE: FLOWERS IN THE
GARDEN, A HUMMINGBIRD FLITTING AROUND, AND EVEN A
PRETTY STONE. The cool grass was a blessing too. Ezra sat down in
it to rest. He picked some grass. He played with it in his hands and
then he discovered something—a four-leaf clover! Ezra ran home to
tell his mommy.

"Look, Mommy. I found a four-leaf clover. I'm lucky! Now
something good will happen."

"The clover is very pretty," his mommy said. "But a thing has no
power. Every good gift comes from God."

People sometimes find a penny or a clover, and they think it
will bring them blessings. But God is the only One who can make
blessings. He blesses people because He loves them.

*Say this little prayer:
"Dear God, I don't need luck;
I just need You. Thank You
for loving me. Amen."*

I Have Talent

*"A person can receive only what is
given them from heaven."*
JOHN 3:27 NIV

A TALENT IS ANYTHING THAT A PERSON DOES VERY WELL.
Jazmin made a list of her friends' talents. She discovered that some
friends could dance. Some could sing, and a few had acted in school
plays. One friend was learning to play the guitar, and another
played the violin. When Jazmin imagined her friends taking part in
the show, she knew that the show would be good.

Danna was very quiet.

"What is the matter?" Jazmin asked.

"I don't have any talent," said Danna. "There is nothing I can do."

"But you are so good at planning things," Jazmin said. "You can
be in charge of the whole show. You can make it all work out."

God blesses everyone with something they are good at. What
special talent has He blessed you with?

⭐ *Name one way that you can
share your talent with others.*

Help me to use my talents
to bless others.

Safety First

Their children play and dance safely by themselves.
JOB 21:11 CEV

GOD BLESSES KIDS WITH SAFE PLACES TO PLAY, LIKE PARKS, PLAYGROUNDS, AND AT THEIR FRIENDS' HOUSES. God is always with His children and watching out for them, but He likes to have grown-ups around to be His helpers too. A place is safe when a trusted adult is nearby to watch and help. Kids should never play alone or in places where there is no one watching. God blesses kids with wisdom to know who His helpers are. His helpers can be parents, teachers, playground leaders, and other people whom moms and dads approve of. Kids should always tell their parents where they will be and which helpers will be with them.

Kids are so special to God. He loves them all. That is why He puts helpers all around them and gives them safe places to play.

Draw a picture of kids playing in a safe place. Put a grown-up in the picture.

143

Freedom

Do not use your freedom as an excuse to
do evil. Live as servants of God.
1 PETER 2:16

IN SOME COUNTRIES, PEOPLE CELEBRATE THEIR FREEDOM—
THEIR RIGHT TO DECIDE FOR THEMSELVES HOW TO BEHAVE.
Freedom is a blessing. God does not hold on to people and force
them to act in the ways He wants. That would be like putting a
butterfly in a jar and taking away its freedom to fly. Instead, God
allows people to choose whether to follow His rules or their own.
Some people use their freedom to do right things and to please
God. Others push God away and make up their own rules. Often,
that gets them into trouble.

God likes it when people choose His way. But He knows that
people are not perfect. When they make poor choices and are truly
sorry, then God blesses them with forgiveness.

*When you say your prayers, thank God for your
freedom. Ask Him to help you make wise choices.*

Thank You, God,
for blessing me with forgiveness.

Fireworks and Fun

Show respect for all people. Love the brothers and sisters of God's family. Respect God. Honor the king.

1 PETER 2:17

GOD BLESSES PEOPLE WITH SPECIAL CELEBRATIONS. In the United States, on the Fourth of July people celebrate their country's birthday. Cities have parades with marching bands and floats. People wear red, white, and blue clothing, the same colors as the American flag. Bands play lively marches while fireworks light up the night. *Boom! Sizzle! Bang!* What fun!

Summer is the season when many countries celebrate their history with special days. People in countries around the world wave their own country's flag and enjoy games and fun. They honor those who serve their countries. They show respect for their kings, queens, presidents, and others.

Without God there would be no countries, no leaders to respect, and no special days. God's greatness is a big blessing! Without Him there would be nothing.

Celebrate God's blessings today. Have a pretend parade with your friends.

Beautiful Music

Sing and make music in your hearts to the Lord.
EPHESIANS 5:19

GOD LOVES MUSIC. He loves to hear His people sing and play music for Him. The Bible tells us:

Shout with joy to the LORD, all the earth; burst into songs and make music. Make music to the LORD with harps, with harps and the sound of singing. Blow the trumpets and the sheep's horns; shout for joy to the LORD the King. Let the sea and everything in it shout; let the world and everyone in it sing. Let the rivers clap their hands; let the mountains sing together for joy.

Psalm 98:4–8 NCV

The words mean that everything God created should praise Him. Music is a lovely blessing. God made it for people to share with each other, and He made it for people to share with Him.

Can you think of a good song to sing to God?

I Use My Voice for God

The Lord's voice is powerful.
The Lord's voice is majestic.

PSALM 29:4

JAZMIN AND DANNA CHOSE THREE FRIENDS TO SING IN THE
SHOW. Each friend had a beautiful voice. The girls knew that the
audience would love their songs.

God's voice is beautiful too. The Bible says that His voice is
powerful and majestic (that means wonderful). Long ago, people
heard God's voice, and they said it is big, like thunder, big like God is.

God blesses everyone with a voice. Voices can be used for
singing, speaking, laughing, teaching, and loving. Best of all, voices
can be used to serve God. Ministers use their voices to preach
sermons about God. Missionaries use their voices to speak about
God to people all over the world. All people can use their voices to
praise and worship God and tell others all about Him.

How will you use your voice today?

 Name three things you can tell someone about God.

*I will shout praises
to bless the Lord.*

Yes, I Can!

I can do all things through Christ because he gives me strength.

PHILIPPIANS 4:13

EVERETT PRACTICED A SONG THAT HE WANTED TO SING IN THE SHOW. He felt fine until he remembered that an audience would be watching him and listening. Then Everett felt nervous. He sang a few notes. Then he stopped singing altogether.

"Everett, what's wrong?" Danna asked.

"I don't think I want to do it," Everett said. "I can't sing in front of people."

"Yes, you can!" said Danna. "I know you can."

When people like Everett are worried that they can't do something, Jesus blesses them with His strength. When people feel nervous, if they set their minds on Jesus, He will come and help them. Knowing that Jesus is there makes people feel stronger and more sure about what they can do.

"Jesus loves you, Everett," Danna said. "You can count on Him to help you."

 What would you say to Everett to help him feel less nervous?

Good manners are a blessing to everyone you meet.

Good Manners

"Honor your father and mother. Love your neighbor as you love yourself."

MATTHEW 19:19

JAZMIN AND DANNA WROTE A LITTLE PLAY ABOUT A KING AND A PRINCESS NAMED ISABELLA. They called their play "Good Manners."

The princess rushed into the throne room. "Father dear," she said. "May I have your permission to attend the grand ball?"

"I am sorry, my child," said the king, "but you are too young to attend."

"But, Father!" said the princess.

"Listen to my words, dear," the king replied. "You may go next year when you are older. I love you, my dear."

"As you wish, Father," the princess said. "I love you too. Farewell."

Jazmin and Danna know that good manners are important and a blessing from God. Well-mannered children obey their parents and speak kindly to them and to everyone else. Jazmin and Danna put the play in their show so other kids would learn about good manners too.

⭐ *How are your manners? Practice good manners with everyone you meet.*

Showtime!

I have depended on you since I was born. You have been my help from the day I was born.

PSALM 71:6

THE TALENT SHOW WAS ABOUT TO START. Moms, dads, sisters, and brothers arrived and were sitting on the ground.

"I'm nervous," said Jazmin. "I hope our show goes well."

"We should say a prayer," Danna suggested.

The girls bowed their heads and folded their hands.

"Dear God," said Danna, "everyone has worked very hard on this show. Please help us do our best. We are depending on You. Thank You, God. Amen."

"And help me feel less nervous," Jazmin added.

Praying made Jazmin feel better. Remembering that God would be helping with the show made some of her nervous feelings go away.

Whenever you feel nervous or unsure of something, say a little prayer. Ask God to bless you with His help. You can always depend on God; He loves you so much!

 Draw yourself performing in Danna and Jazmin's talent show.

All of our blessings come from God.

Good Job!

Do everything for the glory of God.

1 CORINTHIANS 10:31

THE SHOW WENT ON. Danna said a silent prayer before each act. She believed that praying for the performers would help keep them calm.

Everett sang his song without being afraid of the audience. The king and the princess remembered all of their lines. Kids danced to music. Kids sang happy songs. Kids played musical instruments. The audience clapped and clapped and clapped.

"Good job!" Jazmin told her friends when the show had ended.

"We did it!" Everett cheered.

"We did it!" the other kids echoed.

"We did it with God's help," Danna said.

Danna remembered that when you do something good, you should give God the credit. God had blessed Jazmin with the idea for the show. And He blessed all the performers with the talents they shared. Without God, the show would not have happened.

Whenever you do something wonderful, remember to thank God for helping you.

151

A Summer Storm

He made the storm be still. He calmed the waves.
PSALM 107:29

BOOM, CRASH, BANG! Thunder woke Emilio from a sound sleep. Lightning flashed, and Emilio ran to get into bed with his mommy and daddy. "I'm scared," he whispered.

His daddy held him close. "Don't worry," he said. "It's only a summer storm." Emilio's daddy was right. There was nothing to be afraid of because God was protecting them.

God's Son, Jesus, proved that God can calm a storm.

One night, Jesus and His friends were in a boat when a big storm came. The wind blew, the boat rocked, and the friends felt afraid. They had to wake Jesus because He was sleeping. "Aren't You worried?" they asked.

Jesus stood up, and He said to the storm, "Be still!" And the storm went away.

Whenever you feel afraid, don't worry. God is there with you. He will bless you with His protection and love.

Do you ask for God's help when you feel afraid?

Everyday People

Let us think about each other and help each
other to show love and do good deeds.

HEBREWS 10:24

HAVE YOU NOTICED THAT THERE ARE EVERYDAY PEOPLE IN
YOUR LIFE WHO ARE BLESSINGS TOO? Your family members are
around you so much that you might not think of them as blessings.
But they are! They love you just because you're you. Their love is a
blessing. So are the nice things they do for you. If you go to school
and Sunday school, you have teachers in your life. Teachers are big
blessings because they help you learn. The pastor at your church is
a blessing too. He helps you get closer to God.

Think about other everyday people—the bus driver, the librarian,
the crossing guard. All of them are everyday people who bless you
in everyday ways.

*Pray for the everyday people in your life. Thank
God for them, and ask God to bless them.*

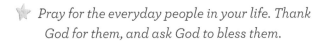

Thank You for rain and thunder
and good summer storms.

153

Water Fun

"I will freely give water from the life-giving fountain to everyone who is thirsty."

REVELATION 21:6 CEV

DO YOU LIKE IT WHEN SOMEONE SPRAYS YOU WITH A GARDEN HOSE ON A HOT SUMMER DAY? Maybe your mommy or daddy turns on the sprinkler and lets you run through it. Water is another fun way to cool off. Some cities have swimming pools where anyone can come to swim. Or maybe you have a pool in your own backyard. If you live near a beach, you can go there to swim in the cool water. Water is a blessing!

Jesus promises water to anyone who wants it. His kind of water is called "living water." Living water is God's love. He gives it away all the time, and there is plenty for everyone. God's love is good and refreshing, like cool water on a hot day.

⭐ *What is your favorite way to cool off with water?*

So Cool

*"Those who give one of these little ones
a cup of cold water because they are my
followers will truly get their reward."*

MATTHEW 10:42 NCV

ON HOT SUMMER DAYS, GOD BLESSES PEOPLE WITH WAYS TO
COOL OFF. Maybe your house has air-conditioning or fans. It feels
better to stay inside where it is cool instead of being outside in the
hot sun. And if you don't have fans or air-conditioning, you can go
someplace that does.

There are other ways to cool off too. Look around, and you might
see people sitting in the shadows of trees or buildings. Shady spots
provide relief from the hot summer sun. And you might see people
trying to keep their bodies cool by sipping an ice-cold drink or
eating ice cream.

God is good! He blesses people with bright, happy sunshine, and
He gives them ways to enjoy it without getting too hot.

*What could you do to help your
friends stay cool on a hot day?*

I am grateful for cool,
refreshing water!

Beautiful Words

Like a fountain of water, the words
of a good person give life.

PROVERBS 10:11

BEAUTIFUL WORDS ARE A BLESSING TOO:

Golden and red trees
Nod to the soft breeze,
As it whispers, "Winter is near;"
And the brown nuts fall
At the wind's loud call,
For this is the Fall of the year.

Goodbye, sweet flowers!
Through bright Summer hours
You have filled our hearts with
  cheer
We shall miss you so,
And yet you must go,
For this is the Fall of the year.

Now the days grow cold,
As the year grows old,
And the meadows are brown
  and sere;
Brave robin redbreast
Has gone from his nest,
For this is the Fall of the year.

I do softly pray
At the close of day,
That the little children, so dear,
May as purely grow
As the fleecy snow
That follows the Fall of the year.

—"A Fall Song"
by Ellen Robena Field

 Use your own words to make a fall poem.

Thank You for
a bountiful harvest.

Farmers Market

You give the year a good harvest. You
load the wagons with many crops.

PSALM 65:11

BRIANNA AND HER MOMMY WENT TO A FARMERS MARKET.
Long rows of farm trucks lined up along the street. Farmers sold fall
vegetables from the backs of their trucks. They had vegetables of
almost every shape and color.

One farmer sold squash: acorn squash, turban squash,
butternut squash, spaghetti squash, Hubbard squash—all kinds of
squash. Another farmer sold pumpkins: orange pumpkins, white
pumpkins, green pumpkins, sugar pie pumpkins, little pumpkins,
big pumpkins, tall pumpkins, fat pumpkins. Other farmers
sold white potatoes, red potatoes, sweet potatoes, and carrots,
turnips, parsnips, onions, and garlic. And sunflowers—big, yellow
sunflowers with their middles full of seeds.

The farmers had worked hard, and God blessed them with a big
crop of vegetables. That is how God loves people—He loves them
BIG. And that is how He loves you.

> *Play Duck, Duck, Goose with your friends, but
> use the words "Pumpkin, Pumpkin, Squash."*

Tender Loving Care

"I am a God who is tender and kind. I am gracious. I am slow to get angry. I am faithful and full of love."

EXODUS 34:6 NIRV

LAURA TAKES GOOD CARE OF HER PUPPY. She treats him with tenderness. *Tender* is a word that means "gentle." Laura is gentle with Scamp. She is kind and understands that Scamp is just a puppy. He has many things to learn. When Scamp misbehaves, Laura tries not to get angry. Instead, she gently teaches him right from wrong so he will grow up to be a good dog.

Laura knows that tenderness is a blessing. She learned about tenderness in Sunday school. She learned that Jesus is tender and understanding. He wants people to be tender with each other and to be good and to love God. That is the kind of person Laura wants to be.

⭐ *Try to be tender all day long. Be gentle and kind to everyone.*

Back to School

*Guide me in your truth. Teach me, my God,
my Savior. I trust you all day long.*

PSALM 25:5

FOR SOME KIDS, THE FIRST DAYS OF AUTUMN MEAN BACK TO SCHOOL. The night before school is for getting ready. Do you have all your school supplies? What will you wear? Mommy and Daddy say, "You have to go to bed now. You have to be up early tomorrow for school."

Back to school makes kids feel a little nervous. That's normal. A new school year means a new teacher, a new classroom, and new friends. Changing from something comfortable and familiar to something new is always a little scary. But change is exciting too. Just think of all the fun you will have and the things you will learn.

God has amazing things planned for you. He will bless you by guiding you and helping you all day long.

 *Have you started school yet? What
is your favorite part of school?*

Puppies are a wiggly blessing!

God Gives Us Teachers

Teach them the right way to live and what they should do.
EXODUS 18:20 NCV

ONE OF GOD'S GREAT BLESSINGS IS PEOPLE WHO TEACH. Without teachers, the world would be a boring place. Teachers show their students wonderful and amazing things. They teach about our world and everything in it. They teach reading, math, science, social studies, and much more.

Did you know that Jesus was a teacher? He taught people about God and how to live right. He gave people instructions about what they should do to please God. Jesus was a gentle teacher. He sometimes used little stories to teach His lessons. He knew just the right words to help people learn. And He loved it when little children came to Him. He loved them just like He loves you now.

Teachers deserve respect. God gave them a special job to do. God blessed them with the talent to teach.

 Make a card or picture to thank your teacher for teaching you.

I am grateful for my teachers and all I learn from them.

I Can Learn

Even a child is known by his deeds, whether what he does is pure and right.

PROVERBS 20:11 NKJV

LEARNING IS A SPECIAL BLESSING. Without it, you could not walk, talk, or do anything else. Learning starts on the day you are born, and it lasts your whole life through. Babies learn to crawl, walk, and eat. Young children learn to count and say their ABCs. Older children learn to add, subtract, tell time, and count money. Kids learn to read, write, and spell. They study caterpillars, butterflies, animals, weather, and magnets. They learn about helping in their communities. And they go on field trips to places like fire stations, museums, and libraries. There are many new things to learn about—and God made them all!

One way to thank God for blessing you with learning is to do your best in school. Learn all you can about His wonderful world.

⭐ *Did you learn something new this week? What did you learn?*

We Can Work Together

All of you together are the body of Christ.
Each one of you is a part of that body.

1 Corinthians 12:27

GOD GIVES PEOPLE THE GIFT OF COOPERATION. Cooperation is something that one person cannot do alone. Cooperation means two or more people working well together.

God had a special helper named Paul. Paul said that cooperation works like a person's body. Think about it. If your brain did not cooperate by telling your body parts to move, you would stand still forever. If both legs lifted off the ground at the same time, you would fall down. If your hand put food into your mouth, and your mouth did not chew, you could not eat. All of the parts have to cooperate.

Cooperation is a blessing. It is a very important gift, and you should use it at school, at home, and wherever you go.

⭐ *Practice cooperating today. Cooperation is a way for people to help and love one another.*

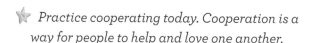

Working together is an important blessing.